Frozen

"I'm crazy about you," Daniel whispered. When she didn't respond immediately, he held her tighter. "Lin?"

Her voice was muffled, but he didn't miss a word. "I'm crazy about you, too."

His heart soared. For the next few minutes, they stood there, frozen, clinging together. Then Lin broke free.

"Why did you do that?" Daniel asked, alarmed.

Lin shook her head. "It's . . . it's happening too fast. We have to take it slower."

"Why?"

"Because that's the way I am." Her eyes implored him to understand.

COUPLES

DON'T GET CLOSE

M.E. Cooper

SCHOLASTIC INC.
New York Toronto London Auckland Sydney

ISBN 0-590-41687-1

12 11 10 9 8 7 6 5 4 3 2 1   8 9/8 0 1 2 3/9

Printed in the U.S.A.   01

First Scholastic printing, July 1988

Chapter
1

Greg Montgomery stretched his arms out lazily and lay down on the sand, letting the hot sun beat directly on his already-bronzed face. After a moment or two, he sat up. The sun was almost too hot.

Even so, it was a perfect summer day. The light breezes of June were gone, but the heavy steaminess of August hadn't set in yet. Tiny wisps of clouds decorated the brilliant blue sky, and the sun glistened on the waves that lapped at the shore. It was the kind of lazy, do-nothing day that made a guy feel like summer was going to go on forever. The turquoise water beckoned invitingly, and Greg debated whether or not it was time for a dip. Decisions, decisions. . . . He closed his eyes and decided to put it off.

"Where's Katie?"

Greg opened one eye and peered at Charlotte DeVries. The pretty blonde in a pink, lace-trimmed bikini had her head cocked to one side, and her smile was flirtatious. It didn't mean anything, though. It was part of her personality.

"She's coming later," Greg murmured. He opened the other eye and looked quizzically at Charlotte's feet. "Why are you wearing shoes on the beach?"

Charlotte giggled. "The sand's too hot. I swear, I felt like my feet were on fire!"

Greg grinned at her southern accent. "Come on, Charlotte, you must have had hotter weather than this in Alabama."

"Oh, it's plenty hot in Alabama," Charlotte replied. "But in the summer we air-condition the whole state." She adjusted the little pink comb that held her hair back from her face. "I'm going in the water. Want to join me?"

"No, thanks," Greg said. "I don't think I have enough energy to make it to the water."

Charlotte made a face at him, but her eyes were dancing with laughter. "Well, suit yourself. But if I drown, you're gonna feel awfully guilty."

Greg nodded toward the water. "Vince is out there. I'm sure he'd be more than happy to rescue you. And if by any chance you require artificial respiration, there's not a guy on this beach who'd mind doing the honors."

Charlotte laughed merrily. "Well, I must say, that's a comfort!"

Greg watched her run daintily down to the edge of the water, and grinned as she ran right in with her sneakers on. She sure was cute. Not his type, of course — she was too much of a southern belle for him. Greg went for only one sort of girl, and her name was Katie Crawford. But Charlotte did seem nice. Beneath her ultrafeminine exterior, she seemed like a pretty solid, down-to-earth girl. As the incoming student activities director, she'd have to be. Greg watched her wade into the surf. He was glad his friends had taken her in.

The whole Kennedy crowd was out in full force today. Greg's eyes roamed the beach where the gang had staked out their summer territory. On one blanket, Daniel was sharing a greasy bag of french fries with Karen. Next to her, Brian was looking restless. He popped open a can of Sprite and called over to Roxanne, offering her a soda, but Rox shook her head.

Daniel was still badgering Karen. Greg couldn't hear their conversation, but he safely assumed Daniel was trying to get some pointers from Karen on editing *The Red and the Gold*. That had been Karen's job until graduation last month, and Daniel would be taking over the school newspaper in the fall when school started.

He'd do okay, Greg thought. When Daniel first transferred to Kennedy, Greg hadn't been too crazy about him. Neither had most of the other members of the crowd. They all thought he was pushy and arrogant. And when he pulled a nasty trick on Karen that almost got her into serious trouble, it created a lot of resentment toward him. But Daniel had turned out all right — he'd even put himself on the line for Jonathan when it looked like Jonathan might not pass English.

On another blanket, Zack was applying suntan lotion to Stacy's shoulders and obviously enjoying the job. He squeezed some more lotion on Stacy's

3

muscular, gymnast's arms. She was Katie's sort-of protégée, and Greg knew Katie had high hopes for her. Of course, Zack was no slouch in the athletic department, either — he'd be the star quarterback of the Kennedy High football team in the fall.

Leaning against a large rock, Jonathan and Lily sat close together, not talking but looking perfectly content just being together. They'd been inseparable since Jonathan had graduated, making every minute count before Jonathan left for college.

Greg could understand how they felt. Katie, too, would be leaving Rose Hill in another month, and the thought made him ache inside. They'd wasted so much time over the past year with all their misunderstandings. Somehow their pride and competitiveness kept getting in the way of their relationship. Well, they were back together now, and there was no point in regretting the past. At least they still had another month together.

Greg's gaze wandered to the solitary figure lying on a towel not far from him. As usual, Rox Easton looked beautiful, her tawny hair floating around her shoulders and her white suit setting off her dark tan. Roxanne still wasn't one of his favorite people, but she was hanging around with him and his friends anyway. Greg had to admit she seemed to have changed a lot since her first months at Kennedy, when she was involved in one scheme after another to become the most popular, influential girl there.

It was funny, though — she'd finally managed to get into the crowd when she started seeing

Vince. And now they weren't even together anymore. At first Greg and everyone had suspected she was only using Vince to get in with them. But lately — today for example — she really looked down in the dumps, and he wondered if it was because she'd really cared about her ex-boyfriend.

Well, he wasn't going to waste a beautiful summer day thinking about Roxanne Easton's romantic problems. He was just glad his own life was back on track again.

Greg looked back at the water. Vince DiMase was just emerging, and he waved to him. The dark-haired, solemn-faced boy ambled toward him.

"You all set for leadership camp next week?" Greg asked as Vince sat down on the sand.

"Yeah, I guess so. I'm still a little surprised that Mr. Barnes picked me to go. I can see why he picked you — I mean, being student body president is a pretty big deal. But I don't know why he chose me."

"Hey, don't sell yourself short," Greg cautioned him. "Taking over the Wilderness Club is no small job. Plus there's all your volunteer work with the rescue squad. Believe me, Barnes knows a leader when he sees one."

Vince looked a little abashed, but he smiled slightly. "Okay, okay, I'm a leader. Or I guess I will be after going to this camp. What goes on there anyway?"

"I'm not sure," Greg admitted. "It's kind of hush-hush. But everyone who's gone to it says it's a great experience."

5

Vince nodded. "I wish I knew a little more about it, though."

"Karen went last year," Greg said. "Maybe she can give us some insight." He turned to look toward the blanket where Karen was sitting with Daniel. It looked as if Daniel was still doggedly questioning her. Brian had managed to escape, going into the water, and Karen was beginning to look a little weary. "Hey, Karen!" Greg called. "Come here a sec!"

She jumped up, looking grateful for the interruption, and started toward them. Naturally, Daniel followed her, determined to learn everything he could from her.

"What's up?" she asked, flopping down on a towel. Daniel planted himself next to her.

"We're talking about leadership camp," Greg told her. "You went last year, right?"

Karen nodded enthusiastically. "It was amazing."

"Why?" Vince asked. "What did you do, exactly?"

Karen thought for a moment. "It really wouldn't be right for me to tell you exactly what we did. You're supposed to go into it with an open mind and without any expectations. If I told you too much it might ruin the experience for you. Besides, you guys probably won't be doing the same kind of exercises we did. I think they try to make them different every year."

"Exercises?" Greg rolled his eyes. "Great, boot camp!"

Karen rolled her eyes. "Ha, ha. Very funny.

Mental exercises; you know, teaching you how to think like a leader."

"You mean, they show you how to give orders, that sort of thing?" Vince asked.

"Not exactly," Karen replied with a sigh. "It's hard to explain. All I can say is, what I learned was really helpful last year in running *The Red and the Gold.*"

"Oh, yeah?" Daniel was looking very interested. "Like, editing skills?"

Karen shook her head. "No, no, it's not about specific jobs like that. It's more about learning to think and organize and get along with a group."

"Teamwork," Greg noted, and Karen nodded vigorously.

"That's it," she said. "There's a lot more to running any organization than giving orders. I don't think my work on *The Red and the Gold* would have been half as good if I hadn't gone to leadership camp first."

"Were there a lot of school newspaper editors there?" Daniel asked.

"Some," Karen said. "There were kids from all kinds of organizations."

"What were the exercises like?"

Karen groaned. "Daniel, I told you, I don't want to give too much away."

"But I'm not even going. You can tell *me*," Daniel insisted.

"How come you're not going?" Vince asked. "Being newspaper editor is a pretty important job."

"Because I was one of the Stevenson transfers,"

Daniel said. "I got here too late in the semester to be considered for the camp." He turned back to Karen. "You think I'm really going to miss something by not going?"

Karen didn't reply. She was looking past Daniel's shoulder. "Hey, here comes Katie," she said.

Greg turned and waved to his girlfriend, who was running toward him. As she got closer, Greg frowned. Something was wrong. Katie looked pale . . . upset. It took a lot to upset Katie.

Greg jumped up and ran to meet her.

"What's the matter?" he asked anxiously.

Gasping for breath, she pushed her long red hair out of her face. "Oh, Greg," was all she managed to get out. Greg could tell she was in a total panic. He led her to his blanket, where the others were watching with concern.

"Take it easy," Greg soothed. "It's okay." He sat down, pulling Katie with him.

Katie took a deep breath, and a little color began to return to her face. "Oh, Greg," she moaned again, "I don't know what to do."

"What's wrong? What happened?"

Katie threw her arms around his neck. Bewildered, Greg responded by holding her tightly.

Finally Katie eased away from him. Her eyes downcast, she studied the blanket as if she still couldn't bring herself to speak.

"Katie, tell me what happened," Greg urged. "Whatever it is, we'll work it out."

Katie took a deep breath. "I had a phone call this morning," she said. "From the University of Florida."

Greg looked alarmed. "They're not taking back your acceptance, are they?" His father had arranged for Katie to be considered for late admission to the university's coaching program, and everyone was ecstatic when Katie got in. A broken leg last year had ended her dreams of becoming a champion gymnast and she had given up a gymnastic scholarship offer at the University of Maryland.

Katie shook her head. "No, I'm still in. But they want me to come down early. They've just recruited a new gymnast, and they want me to work with her."

"But that's an honor!" Karen exclaimed. "They must think you're pretty terrific if they're asking you to come down before school starts. That's great news!"

But Greg suddenly knew why Katie was so upset. He felt a sickening ache as he asked the next question. "When do they want you to come?"

Katie raised a sorrowful face to him. There was pain in her eyes as she replied. "Next week."

Chapter
2

"Next week?" Greg repeated the words and stared at Katie blankly. Then the full significance of what she had said hit him, and he fell silent.

Only Katie sensed his despair. Lily, Jonathan, and Stacy had come over to find out what was going on, and Karen told them Katie's news. While they all congratulated her enthusiastically, Katie just sat there quietly, her eyes dark with worry, and gazed intently at Greg's stunned face.

"That's fantastic!" Lily exclaimed. "I can't believe it! You haven't even started the program yet, and already you'll be coaching!"

Vince nodded in agreement. "They must think a lot of your abilities to invite you up early like that."

"It's a great opportunity," Jonathan added. "If that gymnast is successful, you'll have a real reputation before you even graduate."

"Just think," Stacy said dreamily. "Maybe this gymnast is Olympic material. You could become a world-famous coach."

"And we'll all be able to say 'we knew her when . . .' " Jonathan chimed in.

Greg was barely aware of the conversation around him. All he could think about was the fact that Katie would be leaving in *one week*. After all they'd been through, after all the pain of their separation, they were finally back together and more in love than they'd ever been before. He'd been counting on this summer to make up for all the time they'd lost. It was hard enough knowing she'd be leaving in a month, but now they wouldn't even have that much time together. Only one week. . . .

With a jolt, he suddenly realized they wouldn't even have that one week. He looked at Katie in horror. "Leadership camp!" He was supposed to be leaving on Monday. This would be Katie's last week in Rose Hill, and he wouldn't even be here to spend it with her!

"I know," Katie whispered, reading his thoughts. "Look, I don't have to go. I mean, they didn't *order* me to come. It's my choice. I can say no and just go down there in the fall like any ordinary freshman."

Greg shook his head. "No, you must go. Everyone's right, this is an honor, and it's important for your career. You can't give up a great opportunity like this." He sighed. "I just wish I didn't have to go away to that leadership camp. At least I could be with you for your last week in Rose Hill."

"But you really want to go to that camp, don't you?" Katie asked. "You've been looking forward to it for ages."

Greg shrugged. Suddenly leadership camp didn't seem particularly appealing at all. "I'd rather be here with you," he said simply.

Katie reached over, took his hand, and squeezed it. The mood of the whole group became somber and serious. Congratulations died down and expressions of excitement gave way to looks of sympathy.

"Hey, Monty, that's a rough break," Jonathan said to Greg. "Could you get out of going to that camp?"

"Mr. Barnes selected me, so I guess I have to go," Greg said in resignation. "The school's paying for four people, and I don't think the school can get any money back if someone drops out at the last minute."

"Wait a minute," Daniel said suddenly. "I've got an idea. Why don't I go in your place?"

Greg looked at him doubtfully. "Take my place at leadership camp?"

"Yeah! Look, I didn't get a chance to be considered, and I'd really like to go. Karen said the experience helped her a lot as editor. If you don't want to go, I'll go."

"It's an idea," Jonathan noted.

Greg shook his head firmly. "I can't do that. Barnes picked me, and I agreed to go. It's a commitment, and I can't just back out because suddenly I don't want to go."

"Sure you can," Karen said. "It's not that big a deal to change your mind about going. And I don't think Mr. Barnes would be upset. Last year one of the other kids who was selected canceled at the last minute, and Barnes didn't seem to mind finding a replacement."

Greg still wasn't sure. "Yeah, but won't the camp leaders mind?"

Karen shrugged. "Actually, I remember last year some kids from other schools just showed up at the bus as the last-minute substitutes. Their names weren't even on the list. The camp leaders didn't object. They don't care who comes, as long as they're all willing to participate."

Greg frowned. "I don't know . . . it's so irresponsible of me. If you say you're going to do something, you ought to follow through with it."

"Oh, for crying out loud," Jonathan interjected. "Give yourself a break! Let yourself off the hook for once!"

"Hey, don't put all this pressure on him," Katie objected. "Greg should do what he wants to do."

"And what he wants to do is stay here with you," Lily said. "Right, Greg?"

Slowly, Greg nodded, his forehead creased with lines of doubt. More than anything, he wanted to be here for Katie's last week in town. Who knew when they would have a whole week together again? But he had responsibilities, too, commitments to Kennedy and Mr. Barnes. And he had a reputation for living up to his commitments.

He looked at Katie uncertainly, and she responded with a sad smile. "It's okay," she murmured. "Whatever you decide, it's okay with me. I'll understand."

And she would, too, Greg felt pretty certain of

that. But knowing that wasn't making his decision any easier.

Charlotte lay on her back, letting the heavy salt water keep her afloat as she gazed blissfully up at the blue sky. It was so pleasant here. There weren't any beaches like this back home in Alabama.

Mentally she amended that thought. Alabama wasn't home anymore — this was home. She'd been in Rose Hill for several months, but only in the past few weeks had Maryland started to feel like home.

And the main reason for that was because of all her new friends. Charlotte remembered how she felt when she had first arrived at Kennedy, wondering if she would have a hard time fitting in and making friends. She'd thrown herself into student government work — lots of committees and activities — in an attempt to keep busy and maybe meet some interesting people. Her hard work impressed people, and she was rewarded by being appointed student activities director for the next school year, taking over for Jonathan Preston.

For a while, though, she had wondered if the other kids in top positions somehow resented her being given that job. Jonathan had acted as if she didn't exist and had practically refused to turn over his events calendar to her. Later she'd learned it was nothing personal — Jonathan was just having a hard time accepting the fact that he was graduating and leaving Kennedy.

It wasn't until the night of the graduation bon-fire that Jonathan had finally warmed up to her and given her the calendar. That was also the night she had started hanging out with these friends.

They were a great bunch — the best students at Kennedy — and Charlotte already felt close to them. These days at the beach were wonderful, and the Fourth of July Parade earlier that month had been a blast. And next week she'd be going to the leadership camp. Her life now was almost perfect. The only missing item was a boyfriend, but Charlotte wasn't in any rush to find one. Right now she was having a good time just hanging out with her friends — sharing secrets, problems, and gossip. It was enough for now.

Besides, Charlotte firmly believed that a girl shouldn't go out looking for a guy just for the sake of having a boyfriend. True love had to happen on its own. When Mr. Right came along, she'd recognize him and he'd recognize her. Until then, she'd just have to be patient.

Glancing toward the beach, she saw that every-one was talking excitedly. Something was going on. Charlotte flipped over and swam to shore. Her now-soggy tennis shoes squeaked as she hurried across the sand to the blanket where the crowd had spread their towels and blankets.

"Hey, y'all, what's going on?"

Squinting from the sun, Karen looked up at her. "The University of Florida asked Katie to come down early to start training a gymnast. The problem is, she'd have to leave in a week, and

Greg's supposed to go to leadership camp next week. Which means they won't get to spend her last week in Rose Hill together."

"Oh, no!" Charlotte gasped. "That's awful!"

"I've been trying to talk Greg into letting me go to camp in his place," Daniel added.

Charlotte turned her widened eyes to Greg. "Oh, Greg, you have to take him up on it! How can you even consider going to leadership camp when it's Katie's last week home?"

"Because it's my responsibility," Greg said. He was getting a little testy.

"Who else was selected, besides you and Charlotte and Vince?" Daniel asked him.

"Jana Lacey," Greg replied. "Peter's little sister."

"She's not going now," Charlotte supplied.

Greg looked surprised. "How come?"

"She went to England," Charlotte told him. "She got picked as a last-minute substitute on a student exchange program. She just found out last week, and she left yesterday."

"Did she tell Mr. Barnes she wasn't going to camp?" Greg asked.

"Oh, sure," Charlotte replied. "And he wasn't the least little bit upset. In fact, he was real nice about it. He said he understood and that he even expects things like this to happen because the selections for the camp are made so early and something can always come up to keep someone from going. Barnes is a tough guy, but this isn't school, after all. The camp is extracurricular and totally optional."

16

"Did he find a substitute for Jana?" Vince asked.

"I don't think so," Charlotte said.

"See!" Karen said triumphantly. "You can get out of this, just like I told you."

"Getting a chance to go to England is one thing," Greg muttered. "How can I tell Mr. Barnes I don't want to go because I want to be with my girlfriend?"

Charlotte pushed her damp blonde curls out of her eyes. "Well, you don't have to pour your *heart* out to him. Just let him know that you're missing camp for a really important reason," she said spiritedly. "Honestly, I can't think of anything more awful than not being able to spend your last week together. It's absolutely tragic!"

"And when you drop out, I'll get to go," Daniel added eagerly. "At least you've got a substitute, which is more than Jana had. If Barnes didn't mind about Jana, he won't mind about you."

"Do it, Greg," Karen urged. "You owe it to yourself and to Katie."

"You could make her last week in Rose Hill something fabulous," Charlotte said. In her mind, she envisioned a week of nonstop romance. "Picnics every day, dancing every night — it could be a week y'all can always remember. You'll have all those beautiful memories to keep you warm when you're so far apart."

"And Karen and I will throw a farewell party," Brian suggested. "A major bash. You have to be here for it."

"That's a great idea!" Karen exclaimed. "Okay, Greg, how about it?"

17

Charlotte held her breath as she watched the two of them sitting there, looking at each other. Surely Greg would give in! Couldn't he see the hope in Katie's eyes?

Apparently, he could. "Okay," Greg said happily. "I'll do it. I won't go to camp."

As Katie threw her arms around Greg and planted a noisy kiss on his cheek, Charlotte clapped her hands wildly. She really wasn't the least bit surprised by Greg's decision. She knew if Greg really loved Katie he wouldn't let her down.

"Not only will I stay home," Greg continued, "I'm going to make Katie's last week the best time any person could possibly have."

"Just having you here with me is enough," Katie said.

Greg brushed that aside. "Just you wait," he told her, his blue-green eyes dancing. "You've got a special week ahead of you, K.C." He jumped up. "I'm going to call Barnes right now."

"Are you going to tell him I'm taking your place?" Daniel asked.

Greg paused. "Uh, I don't want him to think we've been making all these plans without consulting him. If you want to go, I think you'd better call Barnes and arrange that yourself."

"Yeah, okay," Daniel said. "I'll call him later."

Vince got up, brushing the sand from his trunks. "If you don't mind, I'll come with you," he said to Greg. "I've got a couple of things I want to ask Barnes."

"Sure," Greg said. He turned to Katie. "You'd

better come, too. I don't want to waste one second of our last week together!"

Katie scrambled to her feet. "Okay," she said, and her eyes sparkled. "I wouldn't mind hearing how you're going to explain why you suddenly don't want to go!"

Greg grinned. "I guess now we'll find out if Barnes has any heart in his soul." He put his arm around Katie's shoulders and they started across the beach.

Charlotte beamed as she watched them walk away. It was all so romantic — just the way life should be. Once again, as always, true love had triumphed!

Chapter 3

Even though she was sitting slightly apart from the group gathered around Katie and Greg, Roxanne Easton overheard enough to figure out what was going on. So Katie was leaving early for the university, and Greg was giving up leadership camp to be with her.

Big deal. Rox couldn't care less about anyone else's romantic problems. She had problems of her own.

It was ironic, in a way, she thought. Here she was, just where she wanted to be. She was with the very best kids from Kennedy High, lying on that very special part of the beach they claimed every summer. One month ago her fantasy, her goal, her one true ambition, had been just this — to be accepted by the Kennedy elite.

Ever since she'd transferred to Kennedy from Stevenson High last fall, Rox had tried everything possible to get where she was now. She flirted with the boys and lied to the girls. She even played one person against another, managing to start up a real rivalry between the Kennedy kids and the transfers. All of this was to get herself accepted by the group — and it was all to no avail. Her schemes and plans had backfired, and before long the crowd seemed intent on excluding her no matter what she did.

Until now. Her work on the Fourth of July Parade had convinced at least some of the kids that she was really okay. And now here she was, hanging out with them. She'd made it. But she'd paid a heavy price to get here. And on this bright sunny day, Rox felt a dark cloud of gloom hanging over her head.

Through half-closed eyes, she watched Vince walking across the beach with Greg and Katie. Her eyes burned as she took in his tanned muscular frame and his broad shoulders, shoulders she had wept on more than once. The lyrics of a popular song from last spring floated through her mind — *when you had him, you didn't want him, and now it's too late.*

Was it too late? Roxanne couldn't accept that. But as Vince passed within a yard of her, he didn't even glance in her direction. And Rox blinked rapidly to keep back the tears. Vince . . . he had been her ticket into the crowd. Well, she didn't need a ticket anymore. She needed him. Her thoughts went back to the day it all began, less than two months ago in the quad at school.

How she must have looked to him that day! She'd just furiously confronted the crowd about why her picture wasn't run in *The Red and the*

Gold's "Leaders" issue. As one of the new year-books' editors, she was definitely a leader, and she felt they'd left her out just for spite.

She'd fled the area after venting her fury, and Vince had followed her. He'd seemed honestly concerned about her plight, and in the next few moments she realized that he was attracted to her.

He wasn't her type at all. He was too serious, too old-fashioned, a real macho kind of guy. Looking back, Rox had to admit to herself that her motives in flirting with Vince weren't exactly honest.

To her, Vince seemed like a real dork — gullible and naive. But he *was* in with the popular kids. She knew she could make him fall in love with her if she played her cards right, and if she was Vince's girlfriend, the others would have to accept her.

So Rox became a damsel in distress; a shy, sweet, fragile female who was "misunderstood." All she wanted was to make friends and find someone to love. Vince fell for her act — and fell hard.

Rox thought about the early days of their relationship. They certainly weren't very exciting. Nature walks and gory stories about car accidents. Ugh! Vince was a total bore at first glance, but she was willing to endure him to get into the crowd. She figured once she was in, she'd dump him and that would be that.

In a million years, Roxanne Easton never would have guessed she'd actually end up falling in love with him.

Through eyes blurred by tears, she watched dismally as the group that had gathered on Greg's blanket began to drift away. Most of them headed into the ocean. Rox briefly debated joining them. It was awfully hot, and a swim might take her mind off things . . . but no, Vince would have to pass her on his way back from wherever he'd gone, and she didn't want to miss him. She clung to the faint hope that seeing her, being reminded of her beauty, would compel him to come back to her.

But remembering the expression on his face that awful day at Frankie's house, she somehow doubted it. As hard as she tried, she couldn't push away the awful memory of his disbelieving face . . . the anger and pain in his eyes. . . .

Suddenly she felt a desperate need to talk about her feelings, to share her heartache. She needed a friend. A few months ago, she could have turned to Frankie. But Frankie wasn't her friend anymore. In her efforts to get into the crowd, Rox had not only lost the single boy she'd ever loved, but her best friend as well.

Her eyes searched the beach for someone to talk to. She wasn't really close to any of the girls. Then she saw Charlotte DeVries coming toward her, and she waved hopefully. Of all the girls in the crowd, Charlotte had been most friendly to her — probably because she was new herself and hadn't heard the horror stories of Roxanne's past. She had been the first to accept Roxanne, and Rox appreciated that. As Charlotte drew nearer, Rox managed a smile.

Charlotte must have seen the gloom in Rox's face, because her expression was sympathetic as she sat down on the sand next to her.

"You look so sad," Charlotte said with sincere concern. "What's the matter?" She sounded honestly interested, and that was all Roxanne needed to prompt her to tell her tale of woe.

"It's Vince," she said, wiping away an honest tear that had managed to creep down her cheek. Roxanne sighed heavily. "Well, as you probably know, we've been going out for a while. Not for that long really, but I thought it was something really special. . . ." She paused before continuing. The next words were so hard to say. "He . . . he broke it off."

"That's awful," Charlotte commiserated. "I didn't know much about you and Vince. What happened?"

"Oh, it's too complicated to explain," Rox murmured evasively. "I guess it was my fault, but it was just a stupid misunderstanding. The thing is — I still love him so much. But he won't come within ten feet of me."

"Have you tried talking to him about it?" Charlotte suggested. "I know it's hard to apologize, but — "

"Believe me, I've tried," Rox interrupted. "I've tried to make up with him at least five times. But he won't listen to me. He won't even look at me!" She looked at Charlotte in despair. "I know he still cares about me — I'm sure of it! But he won't give me another chance! What am I going to do? I love him so much!" The tears began to well up in her eyes again, and this time she didn't even bother to brush them away.

Charlotte put a comforting arm around her.

"Oh, Rox — " she began, but she was interrupted by Daniel, who called across the beach to her.

"Hey, Charlotte! Come here a second!"

Charlotte glanced over in that direction. "Just a minute," she called back.

But Daniel wasn't the type to be put off. Rox saw him get up and start toward them. "Oh, no," she breathed. She didn't want anyone else seeing her in this condition.

Charlotte seemed to understand. "I better go see what he wants," she said. "I'll be right back." She scrambled up and hurried toward Daniel.

Alone with her thoughts again, Rox was glad she'd managed to avoid telling Charlotte any of the details of the breakup. As nice as Charlotte was, she'd probably be horrified to hear what Rox had done.

If only she'd kept her big mouth shut! Working at the Foxy Lady, a designer clothing store, she'd bragged to Frankie and the other girls who worked there about her dull boyfriend and how she was just using him until something more exciting came along. Rox didn't think much of it at the time. Then on the Fourth of July, she and Frankie had spent the morning making sashes for the parade. Since they were running late, Rox delivered the sashes to the gang, while Frankie stayed behind to clean up. Rox had promised to come right back for Frankie, but then the parade started and Roxanne selfishly joined in the marching. Frankie was forgotten. After the parade, there was Vince's family picnic, and that's where the miracle happened: She fell in love.

There, in the midst of Vince's warm, loving family, she saw what she was missing. She saw how the lack of love and affection in her home had made her the kind of person she was — conniving, spiteful, mean. It was as if a blurry photograph had suddenly come into focus. And for the first time ever, Roxanne felt capable of casting the past aside and letting herself love someone.

Just as all this was happening, she remembered Frankie. She raced over to the Bakers' house with Vince, but it was too late. Frankie was furious with her, tired of being used and left with all the work.

In her anger, Frankie really let Rox have it about the way Rox had been using everyone, especially herself and Vince. Only she hadn't seen Vince coming up the walk behind Roxanne. He heard it all. And he hadn't spoken to Roxanne since.

In a way, it was ironic, Roxanne thought. Just when she'd finally found happiness, her past had come back to haunt her. She'd managed to bluff Vince into thinking she was in love with him when she didn't care about him at all. And then, just when she realized how much she *did* love him, just when she knew she didn't have to play any more games, Vince had discovered what she'd been doing.

At least the other kids didn't know exactly what had happened, Rox thought with a shiver of relief. They must have realized by now that she and Vince had broken up, but they didn't know why. Fortunately, Frankie was an honorable ex-best-friend; she'd never gossip. And Vince had too much pride to let it be known how he'd been used.

Roxanne was roused from her thoughts by the sight of Charlotte hurrying back toward her. "He just wanted to know what time the bus was leaving," she told Rox as she sat down by her.

Rox looked at her blankly. "The bus?"

"For leadership camp next week."

"Oh." Rox couldn't even fake an interest. Leadership camp sounded remarkably boring.

"There's Vince now," Charlotte said excitedly.

"You want me to disappear?"

"It wouldn't do any good," Roxanne said dully. Sure enough, Vince walked right past her without even a glance in her direction.

"Oh, Roxanne," Charlotte said softly. "You must feel so terrible."

"If only he'd talk to me," Rox moaned. "If only I could get him alone, make him listen."

"There's got to be a way," Charlotte said passionately. "His foolish pride is standing in the way of true love. It's just too tragic! We have to get you two back together!"

"But how?" Rox asked helplessly. "He's not even going to be around next week. He's going to that leadership camp, too."

"I know," Charlotte murmured. Then she snapped her fingers. "That's it! Leadership camp!"

Roxanne was bewildered. "What about leadership camp?"

"You'll go, too! You can take Jana's place!"

Roxanne was taken aback. "Leadership camp? Me?"

"Sure! Why not?"

"Well, I'm not exactly a school leader. . . ."

27

Charlotte brushed that aside. "That's not important. I'll just call Mr. Barnes and recommend you."

Roxanne looked at her doubtfully. "Leadership camp sounds so boring."

Charlotte shook her head. "Honestly, Rox, it'll be perfect. You'll have plenty of opportunities to get Vince alone. And it will be romantic, too — away from the crowds, alone in the woods — I just know it will bring you back together!"

"Maybe . . ." Roxanne began slowly. She'd gone to computer camp with Frankie last year and had had a brief romance with a Kennedy graduate. She allowed this new spark of excitement to be ignited, and the more she thought about it, the better the idea sounded. She was sick of working at the Foxy Lady anyway, and this would give her a good excuse to quit. And she'd have a whole week to concentrate on winning Vince back.

"I could call Mr. Barnes right now," Charlotte offered. "What do you think?"

Roxanne smiled for the first time that day. The cloud of gloom that had been sitting over her seemed to be drifting away. It was being replaced by a small ray of hope.

She leaned over and gave Charlotte an appreciative hug. "I think . . . that maybe leadership camp might not be so boring after all!"

Chapter
4

Inside the terminal of the Washington, D.C., bus station, teenagers from all over the metropolitan area milled around, clutching suitcases and backpacks. Feeling uneasy, Vince stood near the station entrance, adjusted the straps of his backpack, and tried to figure out what he was supposed to do. He didn't want to have to ask, and feel like a jerk.

A slender, tanned Asian-American girl with long, silky-looking black hair paused as she passed him.

"Are you here for leadership camp?" she asked.

Vince nodded, pleased that the girl seemed to recognize him as a leader type. He started to introduce himself, but she cut him short.

"Check in with the camp leaders," she instructed him. "Over there. Bob and Sharon." With a toss of her head, she indicated a man with a short beard and a petite woman holding a clipboard. They were standing by a door labeled GATE TWELVE, and holding up a sign that read LEADERSHIP CAMP.

Vince wanted to kick himself for not seeing it sooner. "Thank you," he said politely, but the girl was already walking away. Vince admired the way her shiny hair flowed down her back. She was beautiful . . . but not his type. She looked too confident, too sure of herself. She was obviously not the kind of girl who needed a guy to lean on.

No, Vince knew he'd never fall for a girl like that. He liked to be needed. He liked girls who were soft, feminine, fragile. . . . Girls who needed a guy who was strong. For a brief moment a face flashed across his mind. Long, tawny auburn hair, deep green eyes . . . Roxanne.

With all his might, he forced the image out of his head. Thank goodness he was getting away for a while. He needed a break from his painful memories of Roxanne. For the next week, he wouldn't have to see her. Maybe, just maybe, he wouldn't have to think about her, either.

With a determined stride, he walked toward the couple standing by the door. The man, whose name tag identified him as Bob, smiled at him pleasantly.

"Your name?"

"Vincent DiMase."

The woman beside him checked her clipboard. "DiMase, DiMase . . . got it. From Kennedy High, right?"

"That's right."

Sharon smiled warmly. "Welcome to leadership camp."

"Yo, Vince!"

Vince turned to see Daniel ambling jauntily toward him, looking like he went off to leadership camp every day. "This where we check in?" he asked, grinning at Bob and Sharon. He put a hand to his forehead in a mock salute. "Daniel Tackett, reporting for leadership camp!"

Sharon returned Daniel's infectious smile. "Well, you've come to the right place." As she checked the clipboard, Vince couldn't help but shake his head in amusement. Daniel was such a smooth talker.

Sharon looked up, her forehead creased. "I don't see a Tackett here on my list. What school are you from?"

"Kennedy High," Daniel said. "Oh, yeah, I'm taking Greg Montgomery's place. I guess the school forgot to call."

"I've got a Montgomery here," Sharon murmured. "That's strange, though. Usually they call and tell us."

"It's okay," Daniel assured her. "It's a last-minute switch, so that's probably why they didn't get around to calling. There's, uh, no one else listed as a replacement for him, is there?"

Other kids were gathering around them, waiting to check in.

"Well, no, but I suppose it's all right as long as you cleared it with your school," she said hurriedly as she crossed out Greg's name and neatly penciled in Daniel's. "The bus is right through there," she added with a wave of her hand.

Daniel followed Vince onto the almost-full bus

31

and found adjoining seats. Daniel jumped ahead to grab the window seat, throwing his own duffel bag on Vince's seat. Vince took off his pack and stowed it on the overhead rack, then lifted Daniel's duffel bag and tossed it up there, too.

"Congratulations," he said to Daniel as he sat down.

"For what?" Daniel asked. He was busy playing with the lever that made the seat recline.

"For getting Barnes' approval so you could come to camp."

"Oh, yeah." Daniel leaned back in his seat. "Hey, this is pretty comfortable."

"I guess Karen was right," Vince continued.

"Right about what?"

"The camp people don't care if substitutions are made."

"Guess not," Daniel mumbled.

"Did Barnes give you any trouble about it?"

Daniel looked out the window and whistled. "Hey, this might be more fun than I thought. There are some pretty sharp-looking girls getting on this bus."

Vince looked at him curiously. Daniel seemed to be avoiding his questions. "What did Barnes say?" he pressed.

Almost reluctantly, Daniel turned away from the window and faced him. "Not much." Then he grinned. "Mainly because I didn't talk to him."

Vince was floored. "You're kidding! You didn't even ask Barnes if it was okay for you to come?"

Daniel made a face. "To tell the truth, I didn't want to hassle with him, so I told my guidance counselor instead. He'll find out sooner or later, and you know what Barnes is like. I don't think he trusts me. Ever since that business with Jonathan's term paper, every time I see him he sort of looks at me cross-eyed. I have a feeling he's not too thrilled about my being selected as editor of the newspaper."

Vince thought about that. "You can't really blame him," he said. "What you did wasn't exactly ethical."

"Hey, hold on a minute," Daniel objected. "You were in on it, too! Besides, you know I didn't actually write the paper. Jonathan had already done all the background work. All I did was organize his notes and put them together on paper. It was more like typing a paper, not writing one."

Vince nodded. "I know that, but I'll bet Barnes thinks you fixed up his spelling and punctuation. Essays get graded on that, too. Not just content."

With a nonchalant wave of his hand, Daniel brushed Vince's worries aside. "Look, what's the big deal? I just wanted to help a friend, that's all."

"Hey, I'm not saying your motives were wrong," Vince argued mildly. "I'm just saying what you did wasn't exactly right."

Daniel shrugged. "Jonathan ended up turning in his own paper anyway, so it doesn't matter. Barnes never *saw* mine. Anyway, I'm not sorry for what I did. What was important was making sure Jonathan didn't flunk. We wanted him to graduate, so I did what I had to do to make sure he did. The end justifies the means, man. So maybe what I did was a tiny bit illegal, or un-ethical, or whatever. I was trying to accomplish something that was more important — getting Jonathan to graduate. See what I mean?"

"Sort of. . . ."

"Like right now," Daniel mused. "Maybe I didn't get official approval from Barnes. So what? Even though he's not crazy about me, he probably would have said it was okay. Barnes had time to find a replacement, and no one showed up. That must mean no one else had wanted to go, right? Anyway, what's important is that I'm going to leadership camp, and because of this, I'll be a better editor of *The Red and the Gold*. In the long run, it's Kennedy High that benefits. The students will end up with a better newspaper than they would have had if I hadn't gone to this camp . . . and of course it'll look great on my college applications."

Vince thought about it. Daniel did have a point.

"Maybe you're right," he conceded, but before he could go on they were interrupted. A girl in the seat in front of them turned around and faced them. Vince recognized her as the girl who had given him directions in the terminal.

Her eyes were flashing as they darted back and forth between the two boys.

"He's *not* right," she snapped.

Vince was taken aback. "Huh?"

"Look, I shouldn't have been eavesdropping, but I couldn't help overhearing you guys." She focused stern eyes on Daniel. "What you did was wrong. Morally wrong, philosophically wrong, ethically wrong, and just plain wrong."

Daniel looked totally bewildered. "Who are

you? How do you know about Jonathan and the term paper?"

The girl shook her head, and a lock of raven hair fell into her eyes. With an impatient gesture, she pushed it away.

"I'm not talking about that. I'm talking about your taking someone else's place at leadership camp and not getting full approval for it. That sorry old 'end justifies the means' business is a pretty poor excuse."

Vince waited for Daniel to come back with one of his snappy retorts. But to Vince's surprise, his seatmate was silent. He was staring at the girl as if he'd never seen anyone like her before in his life.

The girl didn't pay any attention to Daniel's lack of response and went on. "What about the other kids at your school? Maybe one of them deserved a chance to go to camp, and didn't *know* about the opening. Maybe one of them would have been a better choice. You just took it upon yourself to decide you were the best candidate." She paused for a breath. "And you had no business abusing the opportunity," she finished spiritedly.

Vince's mouth was open. He had never heard a girl — or anyone, for that matter — give a lecture like that to a total stranger. He looked at Daniel again, expecting to see the usual cocky grin, maybe even a smirk.

But Daniel still looked stunned, as if he were totally unable to speak. The girl seemed to take his silence as a sign of victory. She tossed her head triumphantly and turned back around.

35

Vince couldn't help grinning at his seatmate. Daniel was always so sure about everything, the lecture probably did him some good.

"Guess she told you," he said. He figured that once Daniel's shock wore off, he'd be pretty annoyed.

To his surprise, Daniel didn't seem disturbed at all. If anything, he looked positively happy. "Wow," he murmured. "What a woman!"

"What do you mean . . . ?" Vince was starting to ask, when something he saw out of the corner of his eye distracted him. At that moment, the bus doors banged shut, the engine started, and the bus began to pull out of the station. But Vince wasn't aware of anything expect the approach of two girls down the aisle.

One was Charlotte DeVries.

The other was Roxanne Easton.

Vince couldn't believe his eyes. What was *she* doing here? This was going to be his week of solitude, his time for emotional recovery. He'd been looking forward to getting away, to pulling himself back together. And now here she was, the cause of all his grief.

And it only took one glimpse of the tall, slender figure clad in tight jeans and a soft white blouse to bring back the flood of painful memories. How he had loved that girl! His thoughts went back to that moment on the side of the road, the horror he had felt when he saw her standing by that wrecked car, the relief he'd felt when he realized she wasn't hurt. An actual pain went through him as he recalled the way she'd rushed into his arms.

He remembered holding her, comforting her, telling her he would never let her go.

Another image flashed through his mind — Roxanne at his family's picnic, dancing and laughing, so happy just to be there. How beautiful she had looked that day when she told him she loved him.

And then came the worst memory of all. Valiantly he tried to push it away, but his mind had a will of its own. He saw himself, standing a few steps from the Bakers' front porch, hearing the truth. All her tears, her smiles, her kisses — they'd been an act, a big show she'd been putting on. He'd been betrayed, manipulated, used by the girl he had loved.

He stared straight ahead as the girls approached. Keep walking, he thought fiercely, don't stop. But they did.

"Hello, Vince." Her voice was soft, tremulous.

Vince steeled himself and looked at her. He felt a certain satisfaction in the way Roxanne recoiled at his expression. He was trying to look grim, and apparently he had succeeded.

"What are you doing here?" he asked gruffly.

"I'm going to leadership camp," she replied. "I'm taking Jana's place."

Vince nodded and looked away, hoping his action conveyed nothing but total disinterest. Maybe now she'd go on. She didn't.

"Don't worry," she said. "I've got nothing up my sleeve. I'm doing this for myself."

Her voice quavered as she spoke, and her words weren't convincing. Vince couldn't resist glancing at her from the corner of his eye. She looked so fragile, so sweet, her eyes brimming with tears.

Push-button tears, he reminded himself sternly. She can turn them on and off to get what she wants. Resolutely, he turned toward the window, away from her.

Behind him, he heard Charlotte say gently, "Come on, Rox, there are two seats back there." And they moved on.

Vince faced forward again and tried to relax. But it was impossible now.

"Bumpy ride," Daniel muttered as the bus hit a few potholes.

It was bumpy, all right, Vince silently agreed. But he wasn't thinking about the bus. He was still riding the emotional roller coaster he'd been on since the day he met Roxanne Easton.

Chapter
5

"Oh, Roxanne, look!" Charlotte's voice rang out with enthusiasm. "It's so beautiful here!"

Rox glanced disinterestedly out the window as the bus pulled into the driveway. The lush greenery that met her eyes did little to lift her spirits, nor did the colorful flowerbeds that lined the driveway. A large sign proclaimed PINE LAKE CAMPGROUNDS AND CONFERENCE CENTER. Sure enough, there were pine trees all around. And again, Rox felt a pang. She never would have known what kind of stupid trees they were if it weren't for Vince.

And beyond the trees she could see a lake, very blue and sparkling from the sun. She had to admit it was a pretty environment. And she was relieved to see that it didn't look too rustic, like the computer camp last summer that was tucked in the Maine woods. The *boonies*.

They passed some cabins that looked like cute little beach cottages, and pulled up in front of a low, modern building. As the bus parked, everyone started to get up and grab their bags.

"Here we go!" Charlotte said brightly. "I think this is going to be fun."

Rox doubted it, but she managed a weak smile as she rose and pulled her suitcase down from the overhead rack. She and Charlotte joined the crush in the aisle, which slowly surged forward. They were the last to get off the bus, and they stood on the edge of the crowd that had gathered around Sharon.

"If you'll form a line here, Bob will be giving you your cabin assignments and your keys. Once you've found your cabins, feel free to explore a bit, or relax, or whatever. Just be back here at this building at six for dinner and our first meeting."

Rox and Charlotte got in line. "I hope they put us together," Rox said worriedly. She couldn't bear the thought of sharing a cabin with some stranger and having to make chit-chat. As she stood there, tapping her foot impatiently, she caught snatches of conversations around them.

"I'm trying to come up with a good fund-raising scheme," one girl was telling another. "I have to organize next year's senior trip, and our student council's broke."

"Fund-raising's a real hassle," the other girl agreed. "We got some of our local businesses to help out."

In front of her, a boy was talking about his school's literary magazine. "We want to do something really creative. Everyone's sick of the old format. I've got a great staff, so I figure we'll come up with something different."

Rox shifted her suitcase uneasily. What was *she* doing here? The week was going to be pure torture. There was no way she belonged with all these leadership types. But then, way ahead of her in line, she got a glimpse of the back of Vince's head. *That's* what you're here for, she told herself. She pressed her lips together in firm resolve.

Charlotte reached Bob first. "Hi, I'm Charlotte DeVries," she drawled smoothly.

Bob checked his list and then searched through a box of keys with labels attached. "Here you go," he said, handing a key to Charlotte. "You're in cabin fourteen, and your roommate is . . ." He checked the list again. "Jana Lacey. No, wait, there's a substitution for her . . . you're with Roxanne Easton."

Behind her, Rox breathed a sigh of relief. Briefly, she wondered if she could ask Bob what cabin Vince had been assigned to. No, that would be awkward, she decided. She would just have to find out later.

Bob pointed them in the direction of the cabin, and they took off.

"This is exciting," Charlotte chattered happily. "You know, a whole week is a long time. I hope I don't get homesick!"

Rox grimaced. *Homesick!* What a concept! She couldn't imagine being homesick. Just the opposite. If there was one benefit of going away to leadership camp, it was getting out of that sterile town house for a week.

She wasn't going to miss anyone there. And she sincerely doubted they would miss her. Her brother Torrey would take advantage of her absence to play his stereo at full blast, without having to listen to Roxanne's complaints about it. As for her mother . . . well, knowing her mother, she'd hardly even notice Rox was gone.

An image of her mother, with her white-blonde hair and ice-blue eyes, passed across Roxanne's mind. What a mother, she thought sadly. She was so busy with her social life and her boyfriends that she barely seemed to remember she had kids. Rox remembered how warm and affectionate Vince's family was. That was something she'd never known. It was part of what made her fall in love with Vince.

Charlotte caught her expression. "Thinking about Vince?" she asked.

Rox nodded. "I can't get him out of my mind."

"Don't worry," Charlotte said comfortingly. "If it's true love, it'll work out. Love always finds a way."

"I hope so," Rox sighed.

They had almost reached their cabin when they saw Daniel running up toward them. He was out of breath, and he looked a little dazed.

"What's the matter?" Charlotte asked him. "Can't you find your cabin?"

"No, I found it okay," Daniel said hurriedly. "Look, have you seen a tall girl, kind of thin, with long black hair? I think maybe she's Chinese."

Both girls shook their heads and Daniel frowned. "I've got to find her," he mumbled.

"What's her name?" Charlotte asked.

Daniel looked a little abashed. "I don't have the slightest idea, but she's incredible!"

Charlotte laughed. "Why, Daniel, I swear, I think you're in love!"

Daniel flushed slightly, and grinned. "I think maybe you're right." He was clutching a key in his hand, just like the one Charlotte was holding. Roxanne squinted and tried to make out the number on the white tag attached to the key. It was twenty-something.

"Daniel," she said suddenly, "are you and Vince in the same cabin?"

The second the words left her mouth, she regretted them. Now Daniel would know she was only there to chase down Vince, and in his usual brash way, he'd start teasing her unmercifully about it.

But to her surprise, Daniel didn't even seem to pick up on the intent behind her question. "Yeah," he said briefly. "Uh, look, I'll see you guys later." And he ran off, apparently in pursuit of the dark-haired girl.

"That's so sweet," Charlotte said as they approached the door of the cabin. "It's love at first sight! And Daniel doesn't even know her name!"

Rox couldn't figure out what was so sweet about that, but she reserved comment. Charlotte opened the cabin door, and they went inside to their room.

"Oh, this is just darling!" Charlotte exclaimed, dropping her suitcase and clasping her hands together.

"It's not bad," Roxanne had to admit. It wasn't her style, of course, but the room had a certain charm. Blue and white floral-print curtains hung from the four large windows. There was a rag rug in shades of blue on the highly polished wood floor and against one wall were two beds with pale blue spreads. It was all very country-looking.

Rox opened a door, which turned out to be a closet. "Lots of hangers," she said with approval. She tried another door, which led into a spotless white bathroom.

The girls set about unpacking. "I think it would be so romantic if Daniel found his true love right here at leadership camp," Charlotte said.

It dawned on Rox that she didn't know anything about Charlotte's love life.

"Have you got a boyfriend?" she asked curiously.

Charlotte blushed prettily. "No, not now. I *had* one back in Alabama. Bobby was a year ahead of me at school. He played football, and he had the broadest shoulders you've ever seen. He was real cute, too."

"Did you guys break up when you left Alabama?"

Charlotte nodded, a little wistfully. "Yes, we both figured a long-distance romance wouldn't work out. I don't mind telling you, I hated leaving that boy! But, you know what?" She kicked off her shoes, sat down on a bed, and wrapped her arms around her knees. "Now that I look back, I realize I couldn't really have been in love with him."

Roxanne sat down on the other bed and faced her. "Why do you think that?"

"Because I hardly think about him at all anymore. Honestly, Rox, I have to actually concentrate on what he looked like! I mean, if I had truly been in love with him, I should still be absolutely heartbroken this very minute!"

"That doesn't mean you couldn't have been in love with him," Rox said. "You're hundreds of miles away now. And you know what they say — out of sight, out of mind."

Charlotte looked shocked. "Oh, no, I don't believe that at all. I think if you're in love — really, truly in love — it's for keeps. And it doesn't matter if you're a million miles away and separated for years and years, you stay in love with that one person."

"Maybe," Rox said doubtfully. She couldn't quite agree, though. She'd never thought of love as being so . . . permanent. But then she thought about Vince. If there was anyone she'd ever thought she could love forever, it was him.

"I don't know about love lasting forever," she said mournfully. "After all, Vince used to be in love with me."

Charlotte smiled. "And I'll bet deep down inside, he still loves you. True love never dies."

Roxanne got up and paced the room. "But if he does still love me, why is he acting like this?"

"Because he doesn't know he loves you," Charlotte replied. "Men can be so blind. As soon as he accepts what he's feeling, he'll come back to you."

"I hope so." Rox pulled a hairbrush out of her cosmetic case and began brushing her hair. "Have you met any boys at Kennedy you're interested in?"

"Not yet," Charlotte said. "I'm just biding my time, waiting for the magic."

Rox paused with her brush in midair and looked at Charlotte. "Magic?"

"Oh, you know what I mean," Charlotte said dreamily. "You look at a boy, he looks at you — and Boom! It's magic! You can't explain it, but it's there. You're in love, and you know it's for real."

Rox couldn't help rolling her eyes. "Charlotte, you're such a romantic!"

Charlotte raised her eyebrows. "Wasn't it like that for you and Vince?"

Rox almost laughed out loud. She remembered very well what she was thinking when she first noticed Vince. She thought he was a real dork, a macho man with more muscles than brains. It was hardly love at first sight.

But she couldn't tell Charlotte that. She had a funny feeling Charlotte wouldn't exactly approve of the way she had schemed and plotted to get Vince to fall in love with her. So she just shrugged and said, "It wasn't that easy for me and Vince."

But Charlotte wasn't really listening. She was gazing into space, and her eyes were dreamy. "I just know that one of these days I'll meet Mr. Right. And it'll be perfect." She got off the bed and wandered over to a window.

"I don't think I'll be meeting anyone here," she said, gazing out at the scenery. "We'll be so busy with activities and stuff. But it's such a romantic place. Pretty and peaceful . . . I'll bet it's just gorgeous in the moonlight." She turned and

46

smiled brightly at Roxanne. "That's when you should try to get Vince alone — at night."

Rox tossed her hairbrush on the dresser. "That's easier said than done. How can I get him alone in the moonlight when he won't even talk to me? He pretends I don't exist."

"You'll find a way," Charlotte said confidently.

Roxanne thought about Charlotte's words. She'd always found ways before to get what she wanted. There was no end to the devious schemes her mind could concoct. She just needed a plan of action.

"Maybe I could make him jealous," she mused. "I saw some cute boys on the bus. There must be someone here at this camp that I could flirt with. If Vince saw me hanging out with another guy, that just might do the trick."

Charlotte looked dubious. "I don't know if that's such a good idea. I mean, what about the poor boy you're flirting with? You can't just use a person like that. You could really hurt his feelings."

Rox let out a short laugh. She couldn't begin to count the times she'd pulled that number before — What did she care if she hurt some total stranger's feelings? Honestly, sometimes Charlotte was just a little too considerate. But the more she thought about it, the more she realized that making Vince jealous wasn't such a hot idea. Roxanne had to keep making a conscious effort to be good. She'd hurt Vince with her treachery; now it was time to start turning over a new leaf. And it sure wasn't going to be easy. . . .

"I better not try it," she said reluctantly. "Vince has a lot of pride. If he saw me with another guy, he definitely wouldn't try to get me back."

"Besides," Charlotte said, "you shouldn't do anything sneaky. People in love should be totally honest with each other." She glanced at her watch. "Wow, it's almost six. We have to get back to the main building for dinner."

Automatically, Rox's heart started to beat a little faster. She'd be seeing Vince again! She went back to the mirror, did a little fast makeup fixing, and headed out the door with Charlotte.

"I hope Daniel found that girl he was looking for," Charlotte remarked as they hurried along to the main building. "I wonder who she is?"

Roxanne groaned. "Don't worry about Daniel. You've got to concentrate on helping me!"

Charlotte smiled innocently. "I just want everyone to be happy!"

The dining hall was crowded and noisy. Charlotte and Roxanne went through the cafeteria line and got their trays.

"Here's a table," Charlotte said. Rox followed her, looking around for Vince as she went. She spotted him sitting with some guys on the other side of the room. Well, at least he wasn't sitting with a girl.

A couple of other girls joined them at their table. One was a petite, freckled redhead, and the other a tall, athletic-looking blonde.

"I'm Candy Jones," said the redhead, "and this is Diane Delaney. We're from Oak Valley. Where are you guys from?"

"Kennedy High, in Rose Hill," Charlotte told them. "I'm Charlotte DeVries, and this is Roxanne Easton."

Roxanne gave them a thin smile. She couldn't see the point in knocking herself out being friendly to girls she'd never see again after this week. Roxanne could only be *so* good. Instead, she concentrated on her chicken, which was surprisingly edible.

"What do you guys do at Kennedy?" Diane asked.

"I'm going to be student activities director this fall," Charlotte told them. "And Rox is working on the yearbook."

Candy looked at her with interest. "Really? I'm yearbook editor at Oak Valley High."

"Well, I'm not the editor," Rox explained, feeling a little embarrassed. "I'm in charge of the school clubs section."

"Oh." Candy was looking at her curiously, and Rox couldn't exactly blame her. Being in charge of one small section of the yearbook wasn't exactly a leadership position.

"What do you do?" Charlotte asked Diane.

"I'm captain of the girls' soccer team," Diane told her.

"That's great!" Charlotte said.

Diane smiled. "It's nothing to brag about — at least not yet. The team's done pretty badly the past couple of years. In fact, we're just about the lowest ranked in our region. The girls are pretty down about it. That's why I wanted to come to leadership camp. I thought maybe I could learn

49

some techniques to get their spirits up, improve morale, that sort of thing."

Charlotte nodded approvingly. "I wanted to come because my job involves directing a lot of kids, organizing activities, handling responsibility, and delegating authority. It worries me a little. I don't want to come on like some sort of boss, telling everyone what to do."

"I know what you mean," Candy remarked. "I need to tell the yearbook staff what to do, and I'm ultimately responsible for everything. I have to be able to give orders without making them all hate me!" She turned to Roxanne. "Why did you come to camp?"

Rox smiled uneasily. She couldn't very well tell this total stranger she'd come to chase down her former boyfriend. "I, uh, just want to do a good job," she mumbled lamely.

Luckily, she didn't have to say more. Bob, the camp leader, had gone up to the podium. "Could I have everyone's attention, please?"

The noise in the room died down, and Bob smiled warmly. "Hi, I'm Bob Cantwell, and along with Sharon Dunn, I'll be directing the activities during the coming week. We'll be concentrating on developing skills of leadership, cooperation, and teamwork. I hope you're all prepared for a week of hard work."

There were a couple of groans in the room, but Bob didn't look put off. "I'm not saying it won't be fun, too. But you're here to learn more about yourselves and your capabilities, and that requires effort and commitment. It's not going to be easy, but I think you'll find your efforts will pay off.

You kids are among the cream of your high schools' crop, and your schools are depending on you to provide the leadership in a variety of activities. We're here to help you become the best leaders you can be."

A smattering of applause went through the room, and Bob held up his hand. "Hold your applause till the end of the week, please! Now, I want to warn you, you may find that some of our methods are a bit odd. You might even wonder what our exercises have to do with leadership. Hopefully, that's something you'll figure out as the week wears on."

As Bob continued, Roxanne barely listened. She could really care less about this camp for brown-nosing captains and presidents and leaders. Instead, she turned her head slightly to get a look at Vince. He was listening to Bob, and his expression was serious and intense. Just looking at him made her ache inside.

She wanted him back. And if she was going to get him, she'd better come up with some little exercises of her own.

Chapter
6

Greg sat in a booth at the sub shop and examined with pride the sheet of paper in front of him. He'd just finished the schedule, and if he said so himself, it was a pretty professional-looking job. He'd blocked out each day and then divided the days into three general sections: morning, afternoon, evening. The lines had been drawn with a ruler, and each event was neatly penciled into its appropriate space.

He went over it again, studying each notation carefully, and frowned when he reached Wednesday. Tennis in the afternoon, bowling that evening — maybe that was too much activity for one day and not enough romance. He erased "bowling" and carefully printed "videos at home."

He envisioned Katie and himself on the sofa in his parents' den, watching an old movie — something really romantic, maybe a tear-jerker. Yes, a movie at home was much more romantic than bowling.

But Katie loved bowling, too, and this week she wasn't going to be deprived of anything she enjoyed. He scanned the sheet and put bowling into the blank space on Tuesday night.

That still left Thursday night open. Greg stared at the space on the sheet and racked his brain. What else could they do? He'd already included just about everything there was in Rose Hill that Katie liked doing. For the umpteenth time he went over the schedule. There were movies; skating; bowling; dancing; walks on the beach, in the woods, through the park; dinners in Italian restaurants, Chinese restaurants, and one fancy French place. It was all pretty impressive.

Greg marveled at how much a person could pack into one week. But what could he do with that Thursday night?

Then it hit him. The stores at the mall were open late on Thursday night! He was sure Katie would want to go shopping. After all, there must still be a ton of stuff she wanted to get for her dorm room at school.

Happily, he penciled in "shopping." Then he examined the schedule again, nodding with satisfaction. It was a week Katie would never forget. Action, entertainment, sports, romance — it was all there, packed into one solid week of nonstop fun. And they'd enjoy it all together, just the two of them. They'd build up plenty of memories to comfort them during their months apart.

He glanced at the clock. It was almost two —

Katie would be there any minute. She was probably spending some extra time helping Stacy. He frowned slightly. With so little time left, it annoyed him that she wanted to give up a morning with him to help Stacy with the balance beam. But Stacy had probably begged her so much that Katie couldn't bring herself to say no. She was supposed to meet him here at the sub shop when she finished, and he hoped it would be soon so they could get going on the afternoon's activity.

He checked the schedule to see what it was. Right, a drive out to the farm stand to pick strawberries. And tonight was pizza and a movie.

"Hi, Greg."

Greg looked up and smiled when he saw Karen and Brian. They slid into the other side of the booth, and he pushed the schedule toward them. "What do you think of this? I mapped out the whole week for Katie and me."

Brian and Karen pored over it.

"Wow." Brian's voice was low with disbelief. "You guys are going to do all this? In one week?"

"Absolutely," Greg said, beaming. "I'm not letting one minute go to waste." He looked at Karen to catch her reaction. He was a little disappointed to see that she didn't look particularly impressed.

"Good grief, Greg," she murmured, shaking her head.

"What's the matter?"

"Isn't this a little, uh, hectic?"

Greg brushed that comment aside. "It's a lot of stuff, sure, but we want to make every second count. What's wrong with that?"

Brian laughed. "It just seems to me you'd want to take a moment off every now and then. Like a minute here and there to breathe, sleep, just hang out. . . ."

Karen picked up on that. "Take a shower, change clothes, brush your teeth. . . ."

Greg grinned and leaned back. "Okay, okay, I get the picture. I just want to do everything possible to make this week special for her. You guys are still throwing a party Saturday night, right?"

"Oh, sure," Karen said. "That is, assuming you guys can take time off for it."

"It's already on the calendar," Greg said. "Where's it going to be?"

"My house," Karen told him. "I figured we could have a cookout on the patio. Of course, Brian's bringing the music, and we can dance in the basement."

"Great," Greg said enthusiastically. "Katie'll love it."

"Where is she anyway?" Brian asked. "According to this plan, you two are supposed to be picking strawberries right now."

Greg's face fell slightly. "I guess she's still over at the Fitness Center working with Stacy. Now that Katie's leaving early for college, Stacy's freaking out a little at the thought of losing her private coach."

"Well, Stacy's progress means a lot to Katie," Karen reminded him. "You know that. I think Katie gets a lot of satisfaction out of watching her improvement."

"Yeah, yeah, I know." Greg still couldn't help feeling a little disgruntled. "I know it means a lot to her, but it's not something I can do with her. I want us to spend this whole week together. We won't even see each other again until Thanksgiving — maybe not until Christmas." He smiled weakly. "I just hope Katie remembered to tell Stacy she doesn't have any more time to work with her this week."

"No kidding," Karen said, glancing at the schedule again.

"Here comes the busy girl now," Brian noted, waving toward the door.

Greg started to turn, but Karen grabbed his arm. "Here," she said quickly, shoving the schedule back across the table, "Maybe you shouldn't show her this right away. It's a little overwhelming."

Greg just looked at her blankly. Maybe Karen had a point. It would be more fun to surprise Katie each day with all the activities.

He turned to greet Katie, but she had paused at another booth to talk to someone. She was certainly taking her time getting over to him, and they were already behind schedule.

"Listen, you guys," he said to Brian and Karen. "I'd kind of like to be alone with her, so — "

"Say no more," Karen said, smiling. "We get the picture." They were just getting out of the booth when Katie joined them.

"Hey, where are you going?" she asked.

"Oh, we've got things to do," Karen said vaguely. "We'll see you later."

Katie slid into the booth next to Greg and planted a kiss on his cheek. "Boy, am I beat. I must have gone over that routine a dozen times with Stacy."

"You're not too beat to go strawberry picking, are you?" Greg asked worriedly.

"Strawberry picking?"

"Yeah, at Brown's Pick-Your-Own Farm. You always said you wanted to do that someday." He looked at her anxiously, and Katie must have read the expression. She pushed a lock of red hair out of her eyes and smiled bravely.

"Sure, I guess I've got enough energy left to pick a few strawberries. Sounds like fun."

"Then let's get going," Greg said happily. They were just leaving the booth when Matt Jacobs came into the restaurant. When he spotted Greg, he smiled and hurried toward him, waving something in the air.

"Hey, look! I got 'em!"

"Got what?" Greg asked.

"Tickets for the stock car races in Baltimore. Remember, we talked about going last month, but you couldn't go because of leadership camp. Now you're not at camp, and I've got *two* tickets."

Greg vaguely recalled the conversation. "Oh, yeah."

"It's going to be terrific," Matt rushed on. "We'll see some of the hottest cars in the country. And some of the top drivers will be there."

"When is it?"

"This Saturday afternoon," Matt said, showing him the tickets.

"Oh, wow." Greg shook his head apologetically. "Sorry, Matt, I can't make it. This is Katie's last week in Rose Hill, and we want to spend it together."

Matt stared at him. "Every minute?"

Greg nodded proudly. "Every second."

Matt scowled. "You can't take just one afternoon off?" He looked at Katie for support. "You wouldn't kill him if he deserted you for a few hours, would you?"

Katie laughed. "Of course not. Greg, I don't mind if you want to go to the races. It's only one afternoon."

Greg shook his head firmly. "No way. This is our time, K.C. I promised you a week you'd always remember, and that's exactly what you're going to get." He turned back to Matt. "Sorry."

Matt looked a little disappointed, but he shrugged. "That's okay. I know a couple of other guys who might be interested. See you later."

"Let's get going before we have any more interruptions," Greg said. "We're already late."

Katie blinked. "Late? You mean, we have an appointment for picking strawberries?"

"No, no," Greg said hurriedly, practically pushing her out the door. "But we've got a lot to do, and not a whole lot of time. I've planned a month of activities and packed them into one week, so there's no time to waste."

"Sounds great, Montgomery," Katie said weakly.

Greg paused to give her a quick kiss. He knew she was worn out from her workout with Stacy, but he figured she'd recover during the drive. This would be a week she'd never forget.

Chapter 7

Charlotte finished her breakfast and turned to survey the busy, noisy dining hall. As she looked around, she let her eyes rest a moment or two on the various boys in the room. There were some really cute ones there, but no one who particularly impressed her.

Well, she wasn't here to fall in love, she told herself. She was here to learn about leadership. And as Bob went up to the podium, she turned back and gave him her full attention.

"Good morning. As you finish your breakfast, I'd like you to take a moment to go over the schedules that are on your tables."

Charlotte picked up the typed sheet of paper she had glanced at earlier and studied it as Bob continued.

"After breakfast, you'll have twenty minutes to meet, socialize, whatever. Then at nine o'clock there's a lecture, which will be held in the large room down the hall. Sharon will be talking to you about the psychology of organizations, how people interact with and react to each other in a goal-oriented situation. Her comments will be broad enough to apply to whatever type of activity you're involved in back in your schools. Following her lecture, there will be a test."

Groans resounded through the room and Bob grinned.

"Don't worry, it's not a test on what you remember from the lecture. This test will be composed of a series of multiple-choice questions, and they deal with how you feel about running an organization. At the end of the week, you'll be taking the same test again, so you can compare your responses to the ones you gave today. This gives both you and us the opportunity to see how our program has changed your attitudes about leadership."

"It's like those psychological profiles they make you take at school," Diane whispered across the table. "Actually, they can be kind of fun."

"After the test," Bob continued, "there will be a short break. Then you will be broken up into small discussion groups, where you'll have a chance to share your views with each other."

"What if you don't have any views?" Roxanne muttered.

"Shh," Charlotte responded with a smile.

"Then we'll gather back here for lunch," Bob said, "after which you'll be divided into small groups again for role-playing exercises."

"What's role-playing?" Charlotte asked the

others at the table in a whisper. They all looked blank.

Bob must have noticed the puzzlement on some faces, so he explained, "In role-playing exercises, the group leader will establish a situation and assign different parts for each group member to play — president, vice-president, member, whatever. She may also give you some personal characteristics. You might have to pretend you're overbearing, or shy, for example. Then you'll act out the situation in these roles. It gives you a chance to see how you perform and how others perform under certain conditions."

Charlotte still wasn't exactly sure what he was talking about, but she was comforted by the fact that the others in the room didn't look too confident either. She decided they'd probably figure it out as they went along.

"Are there any questions at this point?" Bob asked.

One boy raised his hand. "What's for lunch?"

A giggle went through the room and Bob grinned. "I'm glad to see you have your priorities in order."

Then he grew serious. "In a moment, Sharon will be handing out something to you. No, they're not name tags. They're badges. The badge you receive will be either red, blue, or green. Now, let me tell you at this point that neither of us knows what color you'll receive. When Sharon gets to you, she'll reach into her basket and pull out a badge at random. Whatever color you get, that's the color you have to wear, and that's the color you'll be."

A murmur went through the room, and Sharon studied Bob's face curiously. For the first time, the camp leader looked almost stern.

"There will be no exchanges, no trading, and you absolutely must wear your badge at all times in a place where everyone can see it. These colors signify your individual status here in the group, and they will determine exactly what you're allowed and forbidden to do."

Now the room was silent, and Charlotte could detect a funny sort of tension in the air. Bob went on.

"Those of you who receive red badges are in charge here, and you have full privileges and total control. You can go anywhere you want on the grounds; you can sit anywhere you want in classes; you have a choice of what you want to eat at lunch. You are the head honchos, the rulers. Essentially, you can do anything you want. You're in control; you've got the most power."

Candy, sitting across from Charlotte, shifted uneasily in her seat. "Gee, I hope I'm a Red."

Bob continued. "Now, some of you will be receiving green badges. You people are in the middle. You will have some privileges, but not complete freedom. For example, you are allowed to drink from any water fountain you choose."

"What a great privilege," Diane murmured.

"You also have limited strolling privileges," Bob went on. "You can stroll the campgrounds as far as the creek to the east, and the rose beds to the west. After the Reds have chosen seats in class, you may choose from the seats that are left. However, you may not speak to any Red unless spoken to. If a Red asks you to do something, you're obliged to obey. In turn, you have power over the Blues."

Now his expression really hardened.

"The Blues, however, have absolutely no rights at all. You are far below the Reds and the Greens. You may drink from only one water fountain, the one in the basement of this building. You may not leave the building unless you are told to. If you are ordered to perform certain tasks for others, you must obey. You have the lowest status of anyone here."

His voice rose, and Charlotte thought he almost looked a little threatening. "Finally, the number one rule: There will be absolutely no fraternizing between the different colors, no chatting, no flirting, nothing. You may only socialize with people in your own group. Now, do you all understand the rules?"

No one spoke, and Bob looked satisfied, as if their silence indicated acceptance. He abruptly left the podium, and all eyes turned to Sharon, who was walking through the room with a large basket handing out badges.

Charlotte could hear exclamations of pleasure from people who apparently had received red badges. And she heard some groans of dismay, which she figured came from the kids who got blue ones.

Sharon finally reached their table. Charlotte held her breath as Sharon approached her first and reached into the basket. Well, it could have been worse, she thought as she took the green badge Sharon handed to her.

Sharon went to Diane next. The other girl also received a green badge, and she and Charlotte exchanged looks of camaraderie. At least they'd have each other to talk to.

Candy, the yearbook editor, got a red badge. She looked almost embarrassed to suddenly find herself in a privileged position. As she watched Candy pin the badge to her shoulder, Charlotte was surprised to realize she actually felt a twinge of envy.

Then it was Roxanne's turn. Charlotte grimaced as she watched Sharon hand her a blue badge. Roxanne stared at it in horror, and Charlotte felt distinctly sorry for her.

It's just a game, Charlotte assured herself. And she was about to say this to comfort Roxanne, when she remembered the rule about talking to other colors. She didn't want to get into trouble, so she just pinned on her badge and wondered what this game was all about. It seemed kind of weird.

Throughout the room, kids were getting up, milling around, and checking out each other's badges. Charlotte rose from her seat and wandered around until she spotted Daniel. She was relieved to see that he, too, was wearing green.

"What's this color thing supposed to accomplish?" she asked him.

"I'm not sure yet," Daniel replied. "Hey, have you seen what color badge that girl's wearing?"

"What girl?"

"The one I told you about yesterday, with the long black hair."

"Are you telling me you still haven't found out her name?" Charlotte teased.

Daniel grinned. "Not yet. But I'm going to find out today."

Just then Charlotte spotted Vince, standing with his back to her.

"Hey, Vince," she called. "What color did you get?"

Vince turned toward her, but before he could speak, a girl wearing a prominently displayed red badge looked at Charlotte with annoyance. "You're not supposed to speak to him. He's a Red."

Vince flushed slightly. He turned his head so the girl couldn't see him and gave Charlotte an apologetic smile. In the meantime, Daniel had wandered away, probably in search of the mysterious girl.

All around her, people were looking self-conscious, surreptitiously looking at people's badges before speaking. This is creepy, Charlotte thought. She started to approach a girl she had spoken to the night before, but then noticed she was wearing blue. No good. Finally she went back to her table to find Diane.

She found her standing by their table, holding two trays and trying to balance them. She looked irritated.

"I can't believe this," she told Charlotte. "I was getting ready to carry my tray up to the window, and this guy with a red badge came up to me and told me to take his tray, too."

"What did you say?" Charlotte asked.

"What *could* I say? He's a Red! So I guess I have to do it."

Charlotte picked up her own tray and followed her toward the trash area. "This is very strange. I mean, I know it's some sort of game, and I guess it's probably for a good purpose, but personally, I think it's pretty weird."

"Me, too," Diane agreed. "But I guess we should just play along."

The girls passed Roxanne, and Diane grinned. "Look, she's wearing blue. Let's see if this system really works. Roxanne! Take these trays to the window for us."

Charlotte watched uneasily as Roxanne's mouth dropped open. Diane was giggling, as if to say it was only a game, but Rox didn't look like she wanted to play at all. And she didn't make a move.

Bob was standing nearby, observing the exchange. "You heard what she said. Take the tray! You're beneath her, and you must obey her."

Roxanne's eyes widened, and as she snatched the trays from Diane, her expression was anything but humble. She looked furious. Charlotte had an awful feeling Rox was about to throw the trays in Diane's face.

"Rox," Charlotte pleaded softly, "just play along. It's just a game. Don't make a fuss."

"No fraternizing!" Bob called out. Roxanne tossed him an angry look and marched away.

"Poor Rox," Charlotte murmured to Diane. "I don't think she likes this game very much."

She didn't. In fact, she hated it. And she couldn't figure out the point of all this nonsense.

She, Roxanne Easton, was being made to feel like a slave, a totally worthless nothing. And she didn't know how much longer she could take it.

And what made things worse, it was really screwing up her plans to get Vince alone somewhere. He was wearing a red badge, which gave him one more excuse to ignore her.

On the way down the hall to the lecture, she noticed a very good-looking boy walking alongside her, and she started to think. Maybe she should reconsider her original idea about making Vince jealous. She had to do *something!* She couldn't just sit back and accept all this.

"Hi," she murmured in her softest, sexiest voice. She gave the boy one of her famous, sidelong glances and a serious knock-'em-dead smile.

She had been just about to say "I'm Roxanne," when he cut her off.

"Better not speak to me, Blue," he said coldly, and indicated his red badge. Quickening his pace, he walked on in front of her.

Rox was floored, not to mention mortified. No boy had ever acted like that when he first met her. What was this game *doing* to them?

She went into the lecture hall and went slowly up the aisle, looking for Vince. She knew he wouldn't speak to her, but at least she could make sure she was sitting in a place where he could see her. She'd taken extra pains with her looks that morning. While the other girls had gone "country" — wearing baggy, beat-up jeans and no makeup — Rox had worn tight white pants and a royal blue halter. She'd pulled her hair back with a banana-comb so it cascaded down her neck. She looked great, and she knew it. And she wanted to force Vince to look at what he was passing up.

She was halfway down the aisle when a girl turned to her and called out harshly, "Hey, Blue! You belong in the back of the room!"

In the quiet that followed, everyone else turned to stare at her accusingly. Rox tried to look as proud as possible as she whirled around and walked briskly to the back. There she saw a row of kids, all wearing blue badges. They looked distinctly uncomfortable and downcast. What was she, Roxanne Easton, doing back here with this bunch of losers?

Reluctantly, she joined them, fuming. She hadn't felt this much like an outcast since her first days at Kennedy.

The lecture started, but Rox didn't pay much attention. She was still trying to think of a way to attract Vince. This color business was just making it more difficult.

After the lecture came discussion groups. This time, a cocky, obnoxious boy ordered all the Blues to sit way in the back, in a corner, and they weren't even allowed to participate in the discussion. That part didn't bother Roxanne all that much. She wasn't very interested in the topic in the first place. What really bothered her were the contemptuous looks from the Reds and the Greens. She was beginning to feel like the scum of the earth, and it infuriated her.

Then came the final insult. Bob called out to the group, "We need help serving in the dining hall."

A Red looked directly at Roxanne and said, "You, go with him."

Rox wanted to scream, but she didn't want to be any more embarrassed than she already was. She could read the expressions on the faces of other kids in the group. Some looked disdainful, others were gazing at her with sympathy. Neither were expressions she was accustomed to getting.

Before long she found herself standing behind the counter, a spatula in her hand, turning hamburgers on the grill and taking orders from assorted Reds and Greens. She'd never felt so humiliated in her whole life.

"Give me a hamburger, plain," a boy said. He didn't even bother to say "please." Trying to control her fury, Rox slipped the spatula under a hamburger, slapped it on a bun, tossed it on a plate and handed it to him. The boy looked under the bun.

"It's not done enough. Cook it some more." He thrust it back at her.

Rox wanted to throw it in his face. Being spoken to like this was bad enough. What made it worse was the fact that Vince stood right behind the boy, listening to him. And he didn't seem to care a bit that Rox was in this demeaning position. His expression was stoic and unfeeling.

Roxanne made a fast decision. If there was one thing she knew for sure about Vince, it was the fact that he hated to see a girl suffer. That was how Rox had hooked him in the first place — by gaining his sympathy. There was no way Vince could remain passive if someone was in trouble. That's just the kind of guy he was.

Rox turned around, pretending to put the hamburger back on the grill. Then, with every bit of dramatic ability she could muster, she jumped back and let out a shriek worthy of an academy award. She dropped the spatula, clutched her wrist, and began to cry.

"The grease! It splattered on my arm," she whimpered.

It was a great performance, and it worked. Vince jumped ahead of the guy in front of him and ran around to the other side of the counter.

"Here, let me see your arm," he said in a firm but sympathetic tone. Rox was thrilled to hear the real concern in his voice. But she continued to whimper, keeping her hand firmly over her wrist and shaking her head, as if she were in too much pain to let go.

And then another voice came from behind Vince. "Let's have a look at that," a Red named Charles said. Rox remembered him from lectures — he was a real aggressive guy, always asking questions and challenging Bob. Charles took Rox's arm and pulled her other hand away. He examined the unblemished wrist, felt it, and shook his head.

"Well, it was a noble effort," he said to Rox, "but it didn't work. You were trying to bend the color rules, and you failed. There's nothing wrong with your wrist. I can't blame you for trying, but you didn't succeed."

Then he turned to Vince, and his voice was sterner. "What you just did, coming to her recue, was wrong. You've betrayed the system. This girl tried to trick you into crossing the color line, and you fell for it. You should know better than to trust a Blue. She's only trying to tear down the system that keeps you in power. You don't want to lose your power and your privileges, do you?"

Vince looked stricken. It took him a moment to recover his wits. "I don't know if this is such a good system," he finally said. "I mean, why should we have privileges when other people are suffering? Shouldn't the Blues have some rights, too?"

Charles gazed at him keenly. "But the Blues don't seem to deserve any rights or privileges. Look at this girl. Look how devious and dishonest she was in trying to get your attention. Does a person like that deserve rights?"

Vince stared at Roxanne, and suddenly his eyes were filled with fury. It was as if Charles's words had reminded him of something else.

"No," he said flatly.

And Rox watched in despair as he turned and marched away.

Chapter
8

Daniel ate his lunch quickly, exchanging only a few words with the other Greens who sat at his table. For once in his life, he wasn't in the mood for conversation. When he finished eating, he got up to return his tray. He knew he could have gotten a Blue to do it for him, but he didn't want to. The whole situation was making him uncomfortable. He didn't want any Reds ordering him around. At the same time, he didn't feel like lording his power over the Blues. When he finished returning the tray, he decided to go outside. He needed some time alone, some time to think about this color business and what it was all about, especially after hearing that scene with Vince and Charles and Roxanne.

He left the building and strolled through the wooded area in back of the main building. He remembered Bob telling them that the Greens could only go as far as the creek, and he grimaced.

It was a strange game they were playing, but he was beginning to see the point of the exercise.

It was a lesson in prejudice. To see how people reacted, arbitrary class divisions had been set up. And Daniel hated the way everyone was accepting them. It was disgusting the way the Reds automatically considered themselves hot stuff. And it gave him the creeps to see how the Blues were cowering. They were all assuming kids were inferior or superior, just because of the color of their badge.

It's not right, Daniel thought. It was an unfair system, and someone should do something about it. But what?

He was pondering the possibilities when suddenly his heart started to beat faster, pushing all thoughts of the game momentarily out of his mind. There she was, that fantastic girl. She was sitting on a log by the creek, her long, shiny hair drifting down her back like a black silk curtain.

Daniel made his way over to her, slowly, taking the time to frantically come up with some sort of witty, charming overture. But this time, his creative genius failed him.

"Uh, hi." It was all he could manage, but at least it got her attention. Not much else, though. She turned her head toward him, eyed him coolly, and sort of smiled. But it was a brittle smile, and not very welcoming.

Daniel realized why as he faced her directly. He could see her red badge. According to the rules, he had no right to approach her.

But he knew he wasn't going to let some stupid

73

game stand in his way. "Is there room on that log for two?" he asked.

She didn't reply, but she didn't say no. As he sat down next to her, she continued to gaze at him steadily, without expression.

He wanted to start off with a great opening line, something that would get the conversation going. Usually, he had no problem with that sort of thing. His natural confidence and cockiness had always served him well.

But there was something about this girl that made him hold his brash charm in check. From that brief encounter on the bus, he had a pretty good idea that she wasn't the type to fall for a line. All he could think of saying to her was, "So, what do you think of leadership camp so far?"

Still, she said nothing. And now she wasn't even looking at him. She was staring out at the creek. Was he coming on too strong, he wondered. Or was it simply that she was taking this color business seriously?

She didn't reply, but she didn't get up and walk away, either. Encouraged, Daniel continued. "You don't look like a snob to me. In fact, I have a feeling you're the kind of person who doesn't like this exercise any more than I do."

Her expression actually seemed to soften a bit. At least he knew she was listening.

"Talk to me," he urged. "I know I'm just a lowly Green, but honestly, once you get to know me, I'm not such a bad guy."

A slight smile played about her lips.

"And I really don't want to call you Red," he went on. "Can't we at least exchange the standard information? I'll even go first. My name's Daniel Tackett, I go to Kennedy High in Rose Hill and I'm the editor of our award-winning school newspaper. Okay, now it's your turn."

Finally, the girl relented. "Lin Park, St. Catherine's High, Washington, D.C., head cheerleader of our *undefeated* football team."

"See? That wasn't so hard," Daniel said, grinning happily. "Now, what do you think of this color business?"

Lin eyed him evenly. "What do you care what I think? You're the guy with all the answers. At least, that's how you sounded on the bus."

Daniel's smile faded. "Yeah, I guess I do come off like that sometimes."

Lin cocked her head to one side and looked thoughtful. "You said 'the end justifies the means,' and you believe that, right?" Daniel nodded. "Then tell me, Mister Know-it-all, how does that philosophy fit in with what we're doing here?"

Daniel shifted uneasily. "Well, I guess what they're trying to do is teach us a lesson about prejudice. The Blues haven't done anything wrong, but we have to treat them like they're inferior just because of their color."

"In other words," Lin said, "the point of the exercise is to show how easily people can become prejudiced. The camp leaders' goal is to demonstrate intolerance in action. Well, they seem to have accomplished that. We're all behaving like a bunch of bigots. They've succeeded in reaching their end, so I would assume you approve of this dumb game."

75

Daniel shook his head fervently. "I don't. I think this whole thing stinks."

"Really," Lin said, smiling slightly. "Then what are you going to do about it?"

"Hey, you two!"

Daniel and Lin turned to see Bob hurrying toward them, frowning and shaking his head.

"You're breaking the cardinal rule," the camp leader accused as he faced them. "No fraternizing between colors."

Daniel glared at him. Who did this guy think he was, anyway? The system was wrong, all wrong. A rush of anger went through him. Now he knew what he had to do.

Aware that Lin was watching him carefully, he turned and faced her, his eyes blazing.

"Throw away your badge," he said abruptly. He unpinned his own, got up, and tossed it in one of the two trash bins by the creek. "Now you don't know what color I am. And whatever way you treat me, it will have to be according to the kind of person I am, and not because of my color."

With the first real, warm smile Daniel had seen on her face, Lin unpinned her own badge and threw it into the trash bin. Together, they faced Bob defiantly.

Bob didn't say anything. He just folded his arms across his chest and stared right back at them.

Daniel took the lids off the two trash cans. "C'mon, let's go," he said to Lin. Banging the lids together like cymbals, he marched back toward the dining hall, with Lin next to him and an obviously curious Bob close behind.

With the racket that the two lids made, it

wasn't difficult to get everyone's attention once they were inside the room. Kids stopped whatever they were doing and stared as Daniel and Lin progressed to the podium. When Daniel finally stopped banging the lids, he was gratified to find the room silent, and all the kids watching him with expectant eyes.

"We are calling for a revolution," he stated loudly. "This system is unjust, unfair, and morally wrong! Take off your badges and throw them away. Without any badges, it will be impossible to tell who is a Red or a Green or a Blue. We will all be free and equal!"

Everyone looked startled, but no one moved. Several kids glanced at Bob apprehensively. The camp leader wasn't doing anything to try and stop Daniel.

Lin pounded her small fist on the podium. "All you Reds out there, listen to me. Maybe you like the idea of having special privileges, of being considered superior to others. But if having special privileges means others are denied their rights, then it's not worth having them. If you Reds will take the lead and *give up* control, the others will follow!"

Daniel watched as the kids started looking at each other, and a low murmur could be heard. Then Vince got up from his chair. He unpinned his badge. Holding it up in the air where everyone could see, he crumpled it up.

Suddenly, everyone else was doing the same. And a chorus of shouts and cheers filled the air as everyone took off his or her color badge. Crumpled bits of red, blue, and green paper were tossed in the air. It was like a celebration of freedom. Guys were slapping each other on the back, and a few girls hugged.

Thrilled and excited, Daniel threw his arms around Lin. But the embrace lasted only a second before Lin pulled away from him.

Finally, Bob blew his whistle. The room became quiet, and some kids watched nervously as he bent down and picked up one of the discarded badges from the floor. Then he went up to the podium and stood between Daniel and Lin.

He looked from one to the other. Then a huge smile broke out on his face. "This," he proclaimed, "is leadership. No more badges."

Chapter
9

Katie was lying in bed, her eyes wide open. She was debating whether to get up or not. She'd just gotten a full night's sleep, but she still felt tired. For the past couple of days, she'd been on a nonstop merry-go-round.

Greg had planned a whirlwind of activities for her last week in Rose Hill. Last night, they'd gone dancing at Rockers. She loved to dance, and the evening had been great fun, but sometime after midnight she'd started feeling a little worn out. Greg, on the other hand, seemed full of energy, so Katie had tried to keep up with him.

Maybe that was one of the reasons she was feeling beat. It wasn't just the activities — it was the effort it took to show Greg what a good time she was having. He wanted so much to make her happy, and she wanted to show him how much she appreciated that.

He was so funny about his plans, though. He

was determined to keep to some schedule he'd created but wouldn't show her. Yesterday they were supposed to spend the day on the beach. There had been some unexpected rain, though, and Greg had spent ages going over the schedule, trying to figure out how to rearrange everything.

They had ended up spending the day playing racquetball at an indoor court. Afterward, they were both beat, but Greg had planned to go dancing that evening. And dancing was what they had to do. They'd had a good time, too — after they both got their second wind. Greg was being awfully possessive, though. At Rockers, they'd run into some friends from school — Frankie and Josh and a few others. They were all heading over to an all-night diner for a midnight snack and had asked Katie and Greg to join them. Katie wouldn't have minded. After all, she wouldn't be seeing her friends for a long time, either.

But Greg had said no thanks. He didn't want to share Katie with anyone. It was flattering, and Katie could understand how he felt. After all, Greg was the most important person she was leaving behind. But still, it would have been nice to spend some time with the others. . . .

She gave up on the idea of extra sleep and dragged herself out of bed. Pulling on a robe, she stuck her feet into her slippers and padded downstairs.

" 'Morning, Mom." She glanced at the clock on the kitchen wall. "Wow, is it really ten o'clock? I can't believe I slept so late."

Mrs. Crawford put a couple of slices of bread

into the toaster and looked at her daughter, her eyebrows raised over twinkling eyes.

"Katie, is that really you?" she asked in exaggerated surprise.

"Oh, Mother." Katie took the carton of orange juice from the counter and poured herself a glass.

Her mother smiled. "It's just that we haven't seen you around here much lately. Greg seems to have a monopoly on your time."

"I know." She took a sip of her juice. "He just wants us to spend every minute together before I leave."

Mrs. Crawford eyed her keenly. "You don't sound like you're very happy about that."

Katie automatically went on the defensive. "Oh, no! I mean, I'm happy. Greg's trying to make this week really special for me. He made all kinds of plans so we could fit in everything I like to do. Honestly, Mom, he's been knocking himself out."

"And knocking you out, too, it seems."

"Mom!" Katie groaned. "I can take care of myself!" The minute the words left her mouth, she regretted them. "I — I'm sorry. I guess I am a little beat."

"You *look* a little beat," her mother noted. "I don't think you're getting enough sleep."

"And I've still got so much to do before I leave."

"Have you finished packing your trunk yet?"

"No." Katie gulped down the rest of the juice. "That's what I'm going to do today. I'm going to get started right now."

"No plans with Greg today?" her mother asked.

"I guess we're doing something tonight," Katie told her. "He wants to make each day a surprise, so I never know what he has in mind." A sigh escaped from her lips. "I'm hoping that maybe tonight I can talk him into just sitting around here and watching TV."

Mrs. Crawford nodded approvingly. "It would be nice to see your face around the house for a change. After all, it's not just Greg you're leaving. You're leaving us, too."

"I know, Mom," Katie replied. She gave her mother a hug. "Now, I've got to get going on that trunk."

She had almost made it out of the kitchen when the phone rang. She paused to grab it.

"Katie, hi, it's me."

"Molly!" Katie smiled with pleasure at hearing her best friend's voice. She felt as if she hadn't seen her in ages. "What's up?"

"I was just wondering what you and Greg have planned for dinner this evening."

"I haven't the slightest idea," Katie admitted. "Greg's determined to keep me in suspense every day."

"Well, Ted and I are going to that new Chinese restaurant. The food's supposed to be great, and it's really cheap. You guys want to meet us there?"

Besides wanting to see her best friend, Katie wanted to see Ted, too. Molly's boyfriend had just finished his freshman year in college, and Katie wanted a chance to ask him about it. "I'd love to, but I better check with Greg and see what he's got planned."

"Don't you have any say in what you guys do?"

There was a slight note of disapproval in Molly's voice.

Katie knew what she meant, but she felt as if she had to be loyal to Greg. "Well, he's making such a big deal about our last week together, and he's gone to a lot of trouble making plans. But look, whatever he's got in mind, I'll try to talk him into meeting you instead. I'll call you later and let you know, okay?"

"Great," Molly said. "I know I'll be seeing you at Karen's Saturday night, but it would be nice to have a little time together before you go."

Katie agreed. And as she hung up, she decided she'd insist to Greg that they meet Molly and Ted. After all, it wasn't as if she was asking to spend time away from him.

Back upstairs in her room, she tugged on her most beat-up jeans and an old T-shirt. Then she pulled her long red hair back in a ponytail and set to work. She opened a drawer in her dresser and began going through her things.

An hour later, she was still at it, and the trunk wasn't even half-packed. Decisions, decisions. . . . She was debating whether or not to pack her pink sweater when she heard her mother call out to her.

"Katie! Greg's here!"

Suddenly panicked, Katie tossed the sweater on her bed and glanced in the mirror. She looked awful. She hadn't been up that long, and her clothes were a disaster. Well, too bad, she told herself. If Greg couldn't be bothered to call first and let her know he was coming, he was going to have to take her as she was.

A sudden attack of guilt grabbed Katie as she

realized she was actually annoyed with him. After all, Greg had been doing everything for her. He deserved a better attitude than this.

"Be right down!" she yelled. She pulled the rubber band out of her hair and gave it a few quick brush strokes. It was too bad about the way she was dressed, but she didn't want to keep him waiting too long.

She ran downstairs. Greg was in the living room, tapping his foot and looking at his watch. The way his face lit up when he saw her made Katie feel doubly guilty about having had such negative thoughts. To make up for it she gave him her brightest smile.

"Hi! What's up?"

"Wait till you hear what I've got planned for us today," Greg said excitedly. "How fast can you get ready?"

"That depends." Katie smiled bravely, but her heart sank as she thought of the unpacked trunk in her room. "What am I getting ready for?"

"We're going to spend the whole day in D.C.," Greg said enthusiastically. "When was the last time you saw the Lincoln Memorial?"

"I can't remember . . ." she said, her voice trailing off.

"And I thought we'd hit a few museums — the Air and Space Museum and maybe the National Gallery. Then we could have dinner in George-town."

Despite her resolve to treat Greg well, Katie couldn't bear the thought of spending the day tramping around D.C. What she really wanted to do was pack. But Greg obviously wanted to *do* something. Quickly, she tried to think of an alternative that would make him happy.

"I'm really not up for crowds today," she murmured. "You know, it's the tourist season. All the museums will be crowded. And the restaurants, too."

Greg's face fell, and she went on quickly. "How about a nice walk in the park? It looks gorgeous outside. We could pack a picnic lunch and feed the birds and sit on the swings like we used to do."

Greg's brow furrowed. "But that's what I had planned for tomorrow."

"Well, we can be flexible," Katie replied with forced gaiety. "Park today — " she gulped " — and D.C. tomorrow." She had a strong suspicion she wouldn't feel any more like going into the District tomorrow than she did today, but maybe she could force herself.

"Okay," Greg said slowly, but he still looked a little disappointed. "I guess we could do that."

Katie remembered something. "Oh, and listen, Molly just called. She and Ted are having dinner tonight at that new Chinese restaurant, and they want us to join them. You were saying just the other day that you wanted to try that place."

Greg frowned. "Yeah, but I was planning for us to go there Friday night."

Katie was beginning to feel a little irritated. "What's the big deal? We'll go tonight instead. And we'll do something else Friday night. Honestly, Greg, your schedule's not engraved in stone, is it?"

Her tone was sharper than she had intended, and Greg seemed hurt. "No, it's not engraved in stone. But I wanted to make sure we got to do all your favorite things this week. It wasn't easy organizing all these events, you know."

Katie immediately felt badly about the way she had sounded. "I'm sorry. I know you've worked hard on these plans. And I appreciate it, honest I do. I just thought it would be nice to spend some time with Molly and Ted."

Greg was silent for a moment. "I'd rather spend the time alone with you. But if you really want to see Molly and Ted, it's okay with me."

He definitely didn't sound very enthusiastic about the idea.

"Well, we'll see how we feel later," Katie said vaguely. Why was he making her feel so guilty? "Listen, Greg, if you really want us to spend the day in D.C. — "

"No, no, it's okay," Greg replied hastily. "I can be flexible. This is your week, and we'll do what you want to do."

She gave him a kiss on the cheek. "Let me go change my clothes. I'll be down in a flash."

She went back up to her room and quickly changed into nicer jeans and a clean shirt. He's so sweet, she kept telling herself as she put on a little light makeup. He's doing so much for me, and I do love him. He just wants this last week to be wonderful for the both of us. And it will be.

With a smile that felt like it was stuck to her face permanently, she started back downstairs, hoping she could make it through another "wonderful" day.

Chapter
10

Vince stepped outside his cabin and looked up at the sky. It was a good night for stargazing. For a few minutes, he amused himself by identifying the various stars and formations. It didn't do much to lift his spirits, though.

Well, he couldn't just stand there, but he didn't want to go back inside. The cabin was beginning to feel a little claustrophobic. He didn't know where Daniel was, but ever since he'd stood up to Bob about the color badge business, Daniel had been the camp hero. He'd become the most popular guy there, and he always seemed to have a circle of admirers around him.

Vince headed over toward the dining hall. That was where a lot of the kids had been hanging out in the evenings. Once he was there, though, he didn't feel much like having a conversation with anyone. He located an empty table in a corner, sat down, and pulled out of his pocket a paperback he'd been reading, a James Bond thriller.

But he found he couldn't even concentrate on the action-packed adventure. He had too many other things on his mind. Finally, he gave up and put it down. He just stared into space and contemplated his situation.

If Daniel was on top of the leadership heap, then he, Vince, was on the bottom. Lots of kids were around the other day when he'd tried to come to Roxanne's rescue, and they all heard him get berated. It was a very embarrassing moment. They all probably thought he was a real jerk. He certainly *felt* like a real jerk.

Of course, he hadn't done much to make himself look good. When one of his *own color* criticized him, he had just stood there and taken it. His feeble explanation didn't help matters. He hadn't really tried to defend himself. There he was, with a perfectly good opportunity to blast the system and the camp leaders for making them participate in the stupid experiment. If he had only taken advantage of that, he, Vince DiMase, would be the camp hero now, instead of Daniel.

But he hadn't done it. He'd just accepted what that jerk Charles had said, and had slunk off like a naughty boy while Bob and the whole camp watched him. How could he have been so dumb? He was only trying to follow the rules. He had assumed the badges really meant something, and that he couldn't change anything. It was his own fault that now he felt like a number-one wimp.

But it wasn't *all* his fault. He could still blame Roxanne for putting him in that position in the first place. She had set him up to be a fool, and he'd fallen for it. She'd probably planned it that way, knowing he'd come to her rescue.

Stunts like that were typical of Rox. The way he figured it, she resented the way he'd been ignoring her, and she wanted to get back at him. Well, she'd succeeded. For all he knew, he was the laughingstock of the whole camp.

He was gazing blankly at the door to the dining hall when it opened. Charlotte DeVries stood in the doorway, looking around the room as if she were searching for something.

She is pretty, Vince thought. Her blonde curls were like a frame around her sweet face. He'd never paid much attention to the way girls dressed, but he couldn't help noticing how the soft, embroidered peasant blouse suited her. Even her pale blue jeans looked feminine.

There was something so nice and innocent about Charlotte. Vince didn't really know her all that well, but she had always seemed to be wholesome and refreshing. He was pretty sure she wasn't the type who'd lead him on, only to talk about him behind his back and eventually dump him.

Charlotte spotted Vince in the corner and waved at him. He liked the way she looked pleased to see him. He waved back, and she came over.

"Hi!" she said in her cute, bubbly voice. "What are you up to?"

"Not much," Vince replied. "What about you? What are you doing here?"

"I was looking for Roxanne," Charlotte replied, looking around the room. "Have you seen her?"

"No," Vince replied shortly. "Thank goodness."

The sympathy in her eyes was unmistakable. "Oh, Vince," she said gently, "you're really upset, aren't you?"

Vince just shrugged.

"Tell me what's bothering you," Charlotte urged. "I'm a good listener, and it might make you feel better."

Her voice was like a soft caress. Normally Vince hated talking about his own problems. He always felt a real man should work out his own troubles, without help from anyone. But Charlotte looked so sweet, so understanding, that he couldn't resist.

"I just want Roxanne to stay away from me," he muttered. "I want her out of my life."

"Oh, you don't mean that," Charlotte murmured.

"She really set me up the other day," he said. "She made me look like a total jerk. It's like she's out to get me. She's really screwing up my life, and I just wish she'd lay off."

"Don't be too hard on her," Charlotte said softly. "Honestly, Vince, she wasn't trying to make you look foolish. She loves you. And I think that deep in your heart, you still care for her."

Vince started to object, but Charlotte wouldn't let him.

"She's desperate, Vince. Try to understand. She's so crazy about you, she'll do anything to get you back . . . even if it means doing things she really doesn't mean to. Rox only wanted your attention, that's why she pretended to be hurt."

"It was a trick," Vince said flatly. "That's the way Roxanne operates. She comes up with phony little schemes to get what she wants."

Charlotte cocked her head to one side and smiled pertly. "Well, I shouldn't be letting you in on one of our feminine secrets, but sometimes we girls just do what we have to do to get our men."

Vince couldn't help smiling. She really was cute.

Charlotte leaned in closer, close enough for him to smell her perfume. It wasn't like the heavy, overpowering scent Roxanne used. It was light and delicate, like spring flowers.

"Don't be angry with Roxanne," she whispered. "Try to work things out with her."

Vince shook his head, but he didn't say anything. It was no use trying to explain a person like Roxanne to someone as sweet and trusting as Charlotte. Charlotte probably didn't even know the meaning of the word manipulate.

"I've got to go," she said. "I do need to find Roxanne. Do you want me to give her any message?"

"Just tell her to leave me alone, okay?"

Charlotte looked at him sadly. "I can't do that. She'd be positively devastated. How about if I just tell her you asked about her?"

Before Vince could say anything, she smiled brightly and said, "I'll see you later."

Vince watched as she lightly walked away. So Rox would do anything to get him back. Great. He wondered what kind of dirty trick she was planning right that minute. And he wondered how he could have ever loved her. Why had he fallen for a girl like that? Why couldn't he have fallen for a sweet, honest girl, like Charlotte?

Daniel picked up a pebble and tossed it into the creek. The ripples blurred the reflection of the stars. He'd never been much of a nature enthusiast, but even he had to admit it was a beautiful setting. The moon was bright, and the glimmer of the stars on the creek made it look like diamonds were floating in the water. After another busy day of lectures and discussions and role-playing, it was the perfect place to be. It was peaceful and quiet — and romantic.

That's why Daniel had come there. He was hoping Lin might be drawn there, too. Since their big moment leading the color-badge revolution, he'd seen her around the camp, but they hadn't exchanged anything more than brief greetings. Classrooms and dining halls were no place to talk. He wanted to see her alone.

He'd been sitting on this log, waiting, for over an hour now. As beautiful as the setting was, the log was starting to get uncomfortable. He was about to give up. Then he heard light footsteps behind him and turned around.

"Oh!" Lin looked as if she was surprised to see him. But Daniel didn't think she looked all *that* surprised, and he couldn't help wondering if maybe she hadn't come there for the same reason he had.

"Hi," he said, and indicated the log where he was sitting. "There's room for two."

She sat down — not as close to him as he would have liked, but at least she was there.

"How are you?" she asked politely.

"Fine," he replied. "And you?"

"Fine."

Then they were silent, and once again Daniel found himself trying to think of a way to get a real conversation going.

"You know," he began, "I'm still getting a kick out of the way we handled that color badge business."

Her face became more animated. "Me, too! It was great, wasn't it? I was impressed with the way you stood up to Bob. You deserve a lot of credit."

"But you were the one who actually got the kids to tear up the badges," he reminded her. "I was really impressed with that."

She smiled. "Thanks."

"We make a good team," he added.

Did he imagine it, or did her smile fade slightly?

"You've got a real talent for inspiring people," he continued.

"So do you," she countered. "When you spoke to the crowd, there was real fire in your voice."

Daniel couldn't help but agree. "When I feel strongly about something, I get that way. I can't be lukewarm about things, I get too excited. That's the way I feel about our newspaper at Kennedy, *The Red and the Gold*. I really wanted to be editor, and I would have done anything to get the job." He paused, then added, "It wasn't easy."

"Really? Why?" she sounded sincerely interested, and not ready to verbally attack him like she had on the bus. Daniel found himself telling her everything, straight from the beginning. He told her how he and a bunch of others had transferred from Stevenson High and hadn't encountered much in the way of a welcome.

"There's a bunch of kids that sort of runs things. They're great kids — really involved — and I hang out with them now. But back then, they didn't seem like they wanted us there. Particularly me."

"Why not?"

"I guess I came on too strong with them, especially with Karen. She was the editor of *The Red and the Gold* then. I started telling her how she should run the paper, and what she was doing wrong. And I kept comparing it with my old paper back at Stevenson."

Lin rolled her eyes. "I'll bet she just loved that."

Daniel grinned. "Right. It was pretty dumb of me. Needless to say, she didn't like me too much. Looking back, I can't say that I blamed her. Anyway I could tell she didn't want me anywhere near the newspaper. At the time, some of the other Stevenson kids were having problems fitting in, too. And there was this other transfer, Roxanne. She's here, by the way."

"I think I know who she is," Lin said. "The one who never talks during the discussion groups? Tall, long tawny red hair?"

"Yeah, that's her. She had done some pretty obnoxious things to kids in the crowd, trying to steal boyfriends, that sort of thing. Obviously, the crowd wasn't too crazy about her. The Stevenson kids knew about Rox's nasty reputation, but we weren't aware of what Rox had been doing to the

Kennedy kids. She was trying to get into their clique, and the only way Rox could do that was to start a rivalry between the two schools. She started all sorts of vicious rumors about how the whole crowd was exclusive and was trying to keep us out of their activities. She even convinced me to get back at them for it."

"What did you do?"

Daniel was almost too embarrassed to tell her. The memory still made him uncomfortable. But for some reason, he wanted this girl to know everything about him, even the bad things. And he wanted to know everything about her.

"I talked Karen into interviewing this other transfer, Lily. Lily's a good actress, but Karen didn't know that. And I got Lily to give Karen a made-up interview about how she used to be a runaway, and lived in the streets, that sort of thing. Lily did a great job. She sounded like one of those made-for-TV movies."

"Did Karen believe her?"

Daniel nodded. "She bought the whole thing. She even submitted the finished interview to a college journalism competition."

Lin gasped. "That's awful! She could have gotten into serious trouble if the judges had discovered the story was a fake! How could you have done such a thing?"

Daniel stared at the ground. "I thought it was a joke. I was being a real jerk, I realize that now. Luckily, the interview was 'retracted' before any of the judges saw it."

He glanced at Lin to see how she was taking this. She still looked appalled, but at least she hadn't gotten up and walked away, or berated him as she had before.

Daniel took a deep breath. "Anyway, it took me a long time before I could get Karen to accept my apology and win her trust. But I did, finally. And she was the one who selected me as this year's editor."

Lin was silent for a few minutes, as if she were trying to absorb what Daniel had just confessed. "I don't get it," she finally said.

"You don't get what?"

"Why did you jump to conclusions so quickly? Instead of challenging Roxanne's theories, and trying to find out the truth about the new kids, you automatically assumed they were exclusive and were keeping you out of things. You immediately wanted to seek revenge. Wouldn't it have been wiser to wait and see what was really going on? You could have avoided all these misunderstandings, and you wouldn't have gotten into so much trouble."

Daniel grimaced. "I guess I didn't stop and think; I was too impulsive. That's the kind of person I am. I tend to jump to conclusions and rush into things too quickly. I suppose you could say that patience was never my greatest virtue."

"It's a virtue you should try to learn." Lin's voice carried conviction, but this time she didn't sound as if she was lecturing him. "Sometimes you get a lot more accomplished by being patient, instead of jumping into things."

Something about her tone made him feel as though she was leading up to something personal.

"Are you a patient person?" He couldn't resist

adding, "I have to say, you weren't very patient with me on the bus the other day."

A smile crept over her face. "I know. I try to be patient, but I don't always succeed. But I've learned the value of patience from my parents. It's very important to them."

"What are your parents like?" Daniel asked curiously.

"They're very strict. And they're cautious." Lin sighed. "Sometimes too cautious. They're always worrying about me. They didn't want me to come to this conference. And they definitely didn't want me to be a cheerleader at St. Catherine's."

"Why not?"

Lin shrugged slightly. "They just don't like me to do anything frivolous, and they're afraid of anything new or different. They're very traditional. All they want me to do is work and study. Day and night. Their dream is for me to become a doctor."

"How do you handle them?" Daniel asked. "You must be able to get your way. I mean, you're here."

"Well, I learned to be patient with them. I realized that if I introduced new ideas to them slowly, they wouldn't be so upset by whatever it was I suggested. Now I give them time to get used to an idea before I press it. I never demand anything of them or insist I be allowed to do something. It would only upset or hurt them, and then I'd never be able to do anything I wanted."

"Wow." Daniel whistled. "That must be rough."

"I don't mean to make it sound like they're not good parents," Lin said hastily. "They're wonderful, and I love them a lot. And if I take my time with them and prove to them the values of the things I want, eventually they understand. That's how I became a cheerleader. And that's how I got to come to this camp. If I'd rushed them to make a decision, if I hadn't been patient, I wouldn't be here today."

"Then I'm glad you're patient," Daniel said softly.

They both fell silent, but this time Daniel wasn't trying to think of something to talk about. All he was aware of was the trickling creek, the soft breeze, the moonlight . . . and the pounding of his heart.

He moved toward Lin. When she didn't react, he moved even closer, close enough to kiss her. Slowly, as if she knew what he had in mind, she turned to face him. He put his hands on her shoulders and drew her toward him.

Even though she didn't resist, he felt a tension in her shoulders, as if something were holding her back. Their lips met — and then, abruptly, she pulled away.

She jumped off the log. "I have to go," she whispered.

And she ran off, leaving behind an overwhelmed and confused Daniel.

Chapter
11

Greg was sitting in the lobby of the Fitness Center. What the heck was taking Katie so long, anyway? he thought grumpily. He'd been sitting there waiting for almost forty-five minutes, and he'd looked at almost every old issue of *Sports Illustrated* lying on the table next to him.

He sighed deeply and stared at the magazine in his hands. It was open to an article on professional body-building. There were large, full-color photos of men on the beach with rippling muscles, huge chests, deep tans, and sun-bleached hair. Greg frowned and tossed the magazine aside. What if Katie met a guy who looked like that in Florida? Would she ever dump him for some he-man? he wondered.

Nah, Greg assured himself. Katie was too sensible and down-to-earth. She wasn't the type to have her head turned by some macho, brainless hunk who spent all his time flexing his muscles and staring at himself in a mirror. She'd be bored silly with a guy like that.

But a small element of doubt had planted itself in his mind, and he couldn't shake it. There were a lot of guys in Florida. They couldn't all be brainless and boring.

He looked up at the clock on the wall. She should be done by now, he thought. What was she doing at the Fitness Center today, anyway? Hadn't she known he'd be by for her that morning?

Over an hour ago, he'd gone to her house, expecting to find her ready and waiting for him. Of course, he hadn't actually told her when he'd be there, but he'd been coming for her at the same time every day that week. He'd just assumed she'd be there, ready for another day on the town.

But she wasn't. Her mother told him Katie had gone to the Fitness Center. Mrs. Crawford said that Stacy had called that morning in a panic — something about problems she was having with one of her gymnastic routines. Katie, naturally, couldn't resist her plea for help, and she had gone to the Fitness Center to help Stacy out.

Greg couldn't get too angry at her, though. That was the kind of girl Katie was. One of her finest qualities was her loyalty to her friends, and her willingness to help them. But still, he couldn't help feeling a little annoyed. Shouldn't he come first this week — especially after all he'd done for her? This was their last week together, and they'd vowed to spend every minute of it with each other. Surely Stacy could have worked out her gymnastic problem by herself.

100

"Hey, Montgomery! I didn't know you were a member here."

Greg tossed the magazine on the table and greeted Zachary McGraw, who was showing his membership card to the receptionist.

"I'm not. I'm just waiting for Katie. What are you doing here?"

"Just my regular workout," Zack said, joining Greg on the couch. "Football practice starts in a few weeks, and I've got to get in shape."

"Oh, right," Greg said. "You're quarterback this year." The thought of a new football season starting up didn't do much to lift Greg's spirits. All he could think of was the fun he and Katie used to have, watching the games together. He had a fleeting memory of the two of them, sitting up in the bleachers huddled under a blanket and balancing an umbrella. It had rained through the whole game, but they didn't care. They acted so silly that day, pretending to fight over the umbrella, barely paying any attention at all to the game.

This fall he'd be sitting in the stands alone, Greg thought darkly.

Zack was looking at him curiously. "Something wrong?"

Greg forced a grin. "No, everything's great. I just wish Katie would hurry up. We've got a lot of things to do today."

"You know, we were just talking about you guys the other day at the beach," Zack remarked. "Everyone was saying how we haven't seen you and Katie around much lately."

"Yeah, well, it's her last week in Rose Hill, so

we're trying to spend the time alone together."
Once again, he frowned, thinking of the time they
could be spending together right that minute.

Zack looked sympathetic. "Yeah, it must be
rough knowing you'll be separated. I mean, you
guys have been together a long time. I guess
it'll be kind of weird — Katie in college and you
still in high school. She'll be going to college
football games and fraternity parties, meeting all
these new people, and you'll still be hanging out
at Kennedy High doing the same old stuff — "

"Um, Zack — " Greg interrupted, his voice
unusually harsh. "That's really not what I want to
hear right now."

Zack looked momentarily taken aback by
Greg's tone, but he recovered quickly. "Sorry. I
guess I was out of line. But you and Katie must
have talked about that, huh?"

Actually, they hadn't. For all their time together over the past week, they hadn't really
talked about what it was going to be like when
the two of them were far apart and living completely different lives. It wasn't something Greg
wanted to bring up. This week, they were concentrating on having *fun*. All he wanted to think
about was right now, not next week or next
month. When he thought about Katie being gone,
he got too depressed. And he sure didn't want to
spend their last week together being depressed.

But he shouldn't take his feelings out on Zack,
either.

"Sorry I blew up," he muttered.

"That's okay," Zack replied. "So, what have
you and Katie been up to this week?"

"You name it, we've done it," Greg said expansively. "Tennis, bowling, swimming, movies — it's been great. Yesterday we went to D.C."

"What did you do there?"

"Oh, we were tearing all over the place. We must have hit every sight in town. We even took a White House tour."

"Did you go to the Washington Monument?"

Greg smiled ruefully. "Probably. To tell you the truth, we were running around so much I don't remember exactly what we saw. The whole week's been like that. Everything's happened so fast, it's like a blur."

"Katie must love it," Zack remarked.

"Oh, yeah, absolutely," Greg agreed quickly. But even as he said that, he began wondering. Yesterday, she had seemed a little out of it. She didn't seem to be enjoying the day as much as he thought she would. He brushed the notion aside. It was probably just his imagination.

He looked at the clock again. "I wish she'd hurry up. I planned a lot for today."

"Does she know you're here?"

Greg shook his head. "I didn't want to bother her. She's working with Stacy."

"Oh, come *on*." Zack laughed. "I'm always hanging around and bugging them. That's what boyfriends are for!" he said. "Let's go."

Greg looked around as they walked through the center. The Fitness Center was a part of Katie's life he didn't know much about. During the winter, when crew was off-season, they'd work out together in the school gym sometimes. That was actually where they'd met. But once Katie started training for her gymnastics season, she spent nearly all her time at the Fitness Center. Now that she was coaching Stacy, it was almost as bad.

They passed an area where men and women were lifting weights and then went by a room where people were pushing and pulling on various high-tech weight-lifting machines. Through one glass window, Greg could see some kind of aerobics class going on.

"They're probably in here," Zack said, pushing open another door. Sure enough, there was Katie, with her hands on her hips. Stacy was in the middle of the floor doing flips.

"Stacy, keep your legs straight," Katie yelled. "Get your ankles together! Concentrate!"

"Hey," Greg said loudly, trying to get her attention. Katie glanced over her shoulder briefly and held up a finger, indicating that he should wait. Greg felt like he'd been put on hold.

Stacy spotted Zack, and her eyes lit up the way Greg had hoped Katie's would.

"Hi," Zack said. "Want to work out together?"

"Love to," Stacy bubbled.

"Hold on a sec," Katie said sternly. "I want to see you do that maneuver again. And this time, get it right!"

Greg felt disgruntled. Stacy didn't look all that panicked to him. And Katie didn't seem to be in any rush to get the practice over with so they could be together.

Stacy did her flip again and finally won Katie's approval. Then she thanked Katie profusely and took off with Zack.

"Come on, come on, let's go," Greg said. "I've got another big day planned for us."

Was it his imagination again, or did Katie actually look annoyed before a smile broke out on her face?

"Okay," she said, but her tone was definitely subdued. "Can we go by my house first so I can shower and change?"

Greg sighed. More wasted time before they could start having fun. But maybe it would cheer her up. . . .

"Sure," he said generously. "But just a quick shower, right? No laying around in a big bubble bath. Then I'd have to burst into your bathroom and drag you out." He wiggled his eyebrows at her.

"Very funny," Katie murmured. "Ha, ha." But she really didn't sound at all amused.

Oh, what I would give for a long, hot bath! Katie thought with a sigh. Showers didn't do anything but make you clean. There was no time to relax, to think, to put your mind in order.

Katie jumped out of the shower, pulled on her bathrobe, and ran back to her bedroom to get dressed. Even though she couldn't see him, she knew Greg was downstairs pacing impatiently.

She felt as though her head were spinning. The half-packed trunk in the corner of her room was a glaring reminder of all the things she had to do yet before she could leave for Florida. And it wasn't just the packing. There were all kinds of errands, phone calls, and odds and ends to take care of. She hadn't had a moment alone to do anything. She hadn't even had a moment alone to think. For the past week, by the time she got home at night she was too exhausted to do anything more than take off her clothes and fall into bed. But even sleeping hadn't been restful. There was just too much on her mind.

In just a few days, there would be a dramatic change in her life. She was leaving home and going off to a brand-new environment. There would be new experiences, new people, new challenges. She was excited, but she was also scared.

Emotionally, she still felt pretty unprepared. She wanted to talk about this, to work out her feelings. She wanted to share her confusion with Greg. But she had a good idea he didn't really want to hear it at all. He just didn't want to talk about experiences they wouldn't be sharing.

Besides, there was no time, not with his schedule. He was keeping the two of them on the go from morning to night, rushing from one activity to another, leaving no time to think, let alone actually talk.

He's doing this all for you, she reminded her reflection in the mirror as she brushed her hair. But it was getting harder and harder to act like she was grateful and happy. Next week, they'd be so far apart. There'd never been such a distance between them before. Even during their worst times, their fights, their breakups, they were both still right there in Rose Hill, seeing each other, hoping deep in their hearts that somehow they'd get back together.

But now they wouldn't be seeing each other

for a long time. What would happen to them? she wondered. Would absence make the heart grow fonder? Or would it be more like out of sight, out of mind? Could their relationship withstand such a separation? Could their feelings for each other survive the distance between them? Would they be able to hang on to their love?

There were so many questions. Maybe it would be better if she didn't think about them. They only made her feel more and more confused. What she really needed to do was talk about them — with Greg.

Quickly, she finished dressing and ran downstairs. "Greg," she said breathlessly, "about today — "

"Oh, yeah," Greg interrupted, "I wanted to tell you about my plans. I had to make some last-minute changes in the schedule. Wait till you hear this."

Katie closed her eyes. "Greg, wait, I want — "

But Greg went on as if he hadn't even heard her. "I thought we could go to the roller-skating rink this afternoon. I remember how much you used to love skating. But we're not going to have time to do that now. I hope you're not too disappointed about that."

"I don't want to go skating," Katie said.

"Good," Greg said hurriedly, "because I know you need to do some shopping for your dorm room. I had planned for us to skate this afternoon, then go shopping tonight. But we're going to the mall this afternoon instead, and wait'll you hear why."

He paused dramatically. Here was her chance

to break in, to tell him she didn't want to do anything at all, to tell him they needed to talk. But something in his expression stopped her.

"You know that play you wanted to see at the Arena Stage? The one that's been sold out for ages?"

Katie didn't know what he was talking about, but she nodded anyway.

"My dad got us tickets!"

"That's nice," Katie said. From his expression, she realized he expected a more exuberant response.

"You said you were dying to see it," Greg reminded her.

"I did?"

"Yeah, and my dad really had to beg Mrs. Webster — you know — Woody's mom — to get these seats." He sounded a little injured, and Katie tried to look grateful.

"Anyway," Greg continued, "I figure we'll grab a bite to eat now, then we'll go to the mall and buy everything you need for your dorm room. Then I'm taking you to dinner at a really nice French restaurant. And after that, we'll go to the play. What do you think of that?"

He looked just the way her parents used to look at Christmas, when she was a little girl, unwrapping her presents. His face was proud and expectant. He was waiting to hear cries of joy.

All she really wanted to do was cry, period.

The big housewares store was jam-packed with interesting objects and gadgets. Slowly they walked down an aisle, with Greg pushing a wheeled cart. He spotted a display of hot pots and picked one up.

"This would be good for a dorm room," he remarked. "It's got its own electric cord. You can boil water in it for tea or instant soup."

Katie glanced at it. "Yeah, I guess so."

Greg tossed it in the cart. "What about one of these?" He pulled an item off the shelf and examined it.

Katie glanced at the gadget. "What is it?"

"It's a portable iron. See, you pull this out for the handle, and this part comes up."

Katie nodded. "All right."

Well, Greg reasoned, he couldn't really expect her to get too excited over an iron. He added it to the cart.

"What else do you need?"

Katie shrugged. "I don't know."

"Hey, I'll bet you could use one of those bed pillows," Greg said, pointing. "They're great for when you want to lie in bed and read." He wasn't looking at the pillows, though. He was examining her face for some small glimmer of interest.

"Yeah, maybe." Her voice was vague and unenthusiastic.

What was the matter with her, anyway? Greg was beginning to feel seriously annoyed. Here he'd planned this fabulous day, the best yet, and she was acting like she didn't even care. He'd thought for sure the shopping would make her happy, not to mention the prospect of dinner in a fancy restaurant and going to the theater.

"Well," Greg said, a little impatiently. "Do you want one of those?"

"Huh?"

"One of those pillows! You've got your mother's credit card, and she told you to get anything you need."

"Okay," Katie murmured.

"What color?"

"Oh, green, I guess."

They continued through the store, with Greg pointing out various items and Katie shrugging or nodding. They paid for their stuff and left the store, lugging several large bags.

"There's a poster shop," Greg noted. "You're going to want posters for your walls, right? Why don't you go in there and look around? I need to go in this place next door and pick up something."

"Okay," Katie agreed listlessly. She went into the store, and Greg headed into the one next to it. It was a photography place, and he'd noticed a sign advertising frames on sale. He wanted to pick up a really nice one for Katie, one that she could put a photo of the two of them in.

Greg looked over the variety of frames, but he found it hard to concentrate on them. Katie's behavior wasn't just annoying him. It was making him nervous.

What was going on with her? She was acting so out of it, as though there was something on her mind. In the back of his mind, an awful possibility kept popping up. Maybe she wanted to break up. Maybe she wanted to go away to the U of Florida and forget all about him.

He didn't want to think about it. Just keep busy, he told himself. If you keep moving, you won't be able to think about next week and her leaving.

He didn't want Katie to think about it, either. He wanted to keep her so busy she wouldn't have time to think or make any decisions about their relationship. He wanted her to leave thinking about all the fun they'd had together and counting the days until they would be together again.

Finally, he picked out a frame, bought it, and went back to the poster shop. He expected to find Katie loaded down with rolled-up posters.

Instead, he found her standing in an aisle, her arms empty. She was staring at some awful, babyish poster of kittens.

"You like that one?" he asked in disbelief.

"No," Katie said.

"Then why are you staring at it?"

Finally, she turned and faced him. "Greg, can we forget about this? Can we just go home and talk?"

Greg shook his head violently. "No, there's no time. We've got reservations for dinner, and we've got to get there on time if we're going to eat and make it to the play."

"I don't care about dinner, or the play," Katie moaned. "I wish we could just be normal and hang out with our friends, or just sit around and talk. Greg, can we just forget this is my last week here? Can't we just pretend it's like any other week? I feel like I'm running in circles! I can't take it anymore. I need time to think. I want to be with you, but I need some time alone, too."

Greg suddenly felt panicked. She was leading

111

up to something, he could tell. He didn't know what to do.

"Oh, that's just great, Katie," he said sarcastically. "You know, I've gone to a lot of trouble planning this week. I even gave up going to leadership camp just to be with you. And now you don't even want to see me!"

"Greg, listen to me," Katie pleaded. "That's not what I said. I'm just tired — "

"Tired of what? Of me, maybe?" Suddenly he was really furious. "Well, you can have your time, Katie. I'm going to give you all the time alone you want. How's this? I won't even see you until your farewell party on Saturday night. I assume you're still planning on attending your farewell party. I mean, if it doesn't take too much away from your precious time alone."

Katie's face was red. "You don't have to blow this all out of proportion," she said angrily. "You've totally misunderstood what I'm trying to say."

"I think I understand enough," Greg replied. "Come on, I'm taking you home. Unless you want your time alone to start right now. You could always call your mom."

She hurried along beside him as he walked out of the store and left the mall. In the car, they both stared straight ahead in silent fury. All the way home, Greg wanted to say something. He wanted to ask her why she wanted to be alone, what she wanted to think about, but he was too angry to speak rationally.

And maybe he didn't really want to know.

Chapter
12

The bright, golden rays of the morning sun were like a silent, gentle alarm clock. Charlotte opened her eyes, but she didn't get up right away. For a few moments, she just lay there, enjoying the warmth on her face, savoring the peace and quiet of the country.

It had been a great week. Leadership camp had proved to be even more interesting and worthwhile than she had expected. In the spring, when she'd first learned she would be Kennedy High's new student activities director, she'd felt a little apprehensive about being able to handle such a big job. Now, after the events and activities she'd been involved in over the past week, she felt much more confident.

And she hadn't been homesick at all! Well, maybe a tiny bit the first day or two, but she got caught up in the swing of things right away. Between the lectures and the discussions and all the other activities, there was no time to be home-sick. There were so many new people to meet, so many new experiences, there was no time to dwell on family and friends back home. The week had gone by in a flash. It was hard to believe she'd be going home tomorrow.

She glanced at the sleeping form in the other bed. Poor Roxanne, she thought. Even though she was sleeping, she looked miserable. Leadership camp hadn't been a great experience for her. She hadn't seemed at all interested in the activities. The only reason she had wanted to come was to be with Vince — and he still wasn't speaking to her.

Charlotte felt a twinge of guilt for having encouraged Rox to come to leadership camp, and for planting the hope in her heart that this environment just might bring her and Vince back together. Well, there was still one more day. . . .

She'd better wake Roxanne up, she decided. Rumor had it that the last day's exercise was something major, and they had to be in the dining hall on time.

"Rox," she called softly. When her roommate didn't stir, she got up and went over to the other bed. "Roxanne," she whispered in her ear. When there was still no movement, she nudged her gently.

Finally, Roxanne opened her eyes. For a second, she just stared at Charlotte as if she were trying to figure out where she was. Then the blank expression was replaced by a look of resignation.

"I was having such a nice dream," she said

mournfully. "I dreamed I'd never come to this place."

Charlotte smiled. "Well, you're here," she said briskly. "And we'd better get a move on if we're going to get some breakfast."

Roxanne dragged herself out of bed and went into the bathroom to wash up. "I wonder what kind of fun and games they have planned for us today," she called out to Charlotte. Her tone clearly indicated that she didn't expect whatever activity was planned to be fun at all.

"I haven't the slightest idea," Charlotte replied, running a comb through her blonde curls. "But since it's the last day, I'll bet it's a biggie."

She was right. Thirty minutes later, as she heard the camp leaders describe the exercise, she marveled at how cleverly Bob and Sharon had planned the program. It was the perfect last-day assignment.

"All this week," Bob was saying, "we've been emphasizing teamwork as the best way to get anything accomplished. Being a leader involves learning how to work together in a group situation. Today you'll have the opportunity to see your new teamwork skills in action. For our last major exercise, you're going on an expedition."

"Goody, goody," Roxanne murmured. Charlotte didn't respond. She was starting to get just a tiny bit tired of her friend's constant complaining.

"You will be divided into teams of four," Bob continued, "and each group will receive a compass, a map, and a set of clues. Each team will

115

start off from a different point at the perimeter of the woods, but your goal is to reach a common destination, which is marked on your maps."

"What's the point?" someone called out.

"It's a test of leadership," Bob replied. "The object is to work together within your group to find the swiftest, most effective route to the goal. There's only one rule: You must stay in your group; you cannot split up. In determining your route, you must come to a group consensus, and you have to reach the goal together. The winning team is the group that reaches the common destination first."

A murmur went through the room, and Charlotte could sense that the others were feeling the same way she did. This could really be fun.

"We're going to let you form your own groups," Bob said. "As soon as you've done that, we'll start handing out the materials."

Charlotte noticed that suddenly Roxanne was looking more interested. Her eyes were searching the room. "I have to get on Vince's team," she told Charlotte urgently. "This could be my last chance!"

"That's a good idea," Charlotte told her. "With such a small team, he'll have to talk to you." She looked around. "There he is, over there, in the back."

Roxanne fumbled in her pocketbook and pulled out a mirror. "How does my hair look?" she asked worriedly.

"You look fine," Charlotte assured her.

Roxanne gave her a grateful smile. "Wish me

luck," she murmured, and took off in Vince's direction.

Diane came up to Charlotte. "We've got three in our group already," she told Charlotte. "Do you want to be on our team, or do you have to stay with Roxanne?"

"She's going on another team," Charlotte told her. "Count me in."

Throughout the room, the kids were joining together to form their groups. Charlotte followed Diane to join Candy and a boy from Baltimore. A few seconds later, a dejected Roxanne approached them.

"What happened?" Charlotte asked her.

"I asked Vince if I could be on his team," she said bitterly. "From the way he acted, you would have thought I'd asked him to marry me. All he said was, 'We've already got four.' He wouldn't even look at me."

"That's too bad," Charlotte said sympathetically.

"So I guess I'll have to go with you guys," Rox said with an obvious lack of enthusiasm.

"We've got our team already," Diane told her. "Sorry."

Charlotte felt awful. Secretly she was glad not to have Roxanne on their team. She had a pretty good suspicion her friend wouldn't be much help. But at the same time, she hated to see her looking so depressed. As much as she wanted to stay with Diane and the others, she was about to volunteer to leave the team, when Bob clapped to get everyone's attention.

"We've got one team here with only three people," he called out. "They need a fourth. Is there anyone who hasn't joined a team yet?"

Roxanne raised her arm in a halfhearted gesture. At least that horrible boy Charles wasn't in this group. "See you later," she murmured to Charlotte as she went off to meet her other three teammates.

Poor Rox, Charlotte thought. She looked totally devastated. But there wasn't time to worry about her now. Sharon had just handed Diane their team's map, and she joined the others to examine it.

Daniel's eyes followed Lin as she walked over to two boys from Leesburg Academy. Smart move, he thought. A military school education probably included learning to follow maps and use a compass. They'd be good guys to have on a team. But even if it hadn't been such a smart move, he'd have followed her anyway.

"Need a fourth?" he asked them. Out of the corner of his eye, he tried to read Lin's expression. She didn't look displeased to have him there.

They got their map and equipment from Sharon, and a few seconds later, Bob blew a whistle. "You may begin," he announced.

Daniel, Lin, and the two cadets headed over to their starting point — which turned out to be the little clearing by the creek where Daniel and Lin had sat and talked, and kissed. He glanced at her to see if she'd show any reaction, but her face was expressionless.

Since that evening on the log, they'd talked to each other about their lives. They were getting to know each other better every day. But every time Daniel had tried to get closer — and especially when he tried to kiss her — Lin held back.

The two cadets examined their map and immediately began to disagree over the best way to start out. Daniel started to wonder if their military training was going to be as useful as he had thought it would be.

"Let me see the map," he said. One of the cadets handed it to him without any objection.

Daniel looked at the map with Lin. "What do you think of this?" he asked her. "We'll start out by following this trail and then veer off here."

Lin studied the map. "I don't know if that's the best way," she said. "It seems to me that if we do that, we'll run into this gully. Why don't we turn off here, instead, and we can avoid it."

Daniel gazed at her with undisguised admiration. "Good idea," he said. He turned to the cadets. "What do you guys think?"

They both nodded in unison. If nothing else, they obviously recognized the ring of authority when they heard it, and like good soldiers, they were ready to obey.

The four of them set off. The cadets did turn out to be good map readers, and they were comfortable using the compass. But Daniel and Lin became the actual leaders of the expedition. Daniel wasn't at all surprised by the ease with which they both took command of the group. It was as if their minds were in sync, operating on the same level of intelligence and ingenuity. Now if only their hearts could cooperate so easily, Daniel thought.

They made good progress, and they hit the halfway point even sooner than Daniel had anticipated. They could actually afford to lose some time. Daniel decided to take advantage of the situation.

He *had* to get Lin alone. All he needed was a chance to get her to let her guard down. He knew that, deep inside, she must be feeling something akin to the way he was feeling. And this might be their last opportunity. Tonight there would be a big, all-camp meeting, and there would be no time for romance. It was now or never.

They reached a clearing surrounded by dense patches of woods. Lin was preoccupied with the compass, and Daniel took one of the cadets aside.

"How about doing a little reconnaissance work?" he asked. The boy looked at him curiously, and Daniel explained.

"We've got two options here." With his finger he traced a route on the map. "I think you guys should check out this area and see if it's maneuverable. Lin and I will go in this direction. We'll meet back here in ten minutes and decide which is the best way to proceed. Okay?"

The cadet agreed. He motioned to his friend, and they took off.

Daniel looked at Lin, who was still working with the compass. He wanted to grab her in his arms, hold her tightly, and kiss her. But he couldn't rush her. He had to proceed carefully, cautiously.

He didn't want to risk losing her.

"Can we stop here and rest?" Roxanne asked.

A heavy-set boy with a crew cut looked at her in annoyance. "We just rested five minutes ago."

"But I'm tired," Rox whined. "Honestly, if I take one more step, I'm going to collapse."

Her teammates looked at each other. Roxanne could read their expressions. They were sick of her whining, her complaining, her endless pleas for time to rest. She was pretty sure they would be more than happy to leave her behind to fend for herself. She didn't care. She would just as soon let them leave her behind.

She couldn't stand much more of this. She was bored and tired and depressed. She couldn't care less whether or not they won this stupid game.

"You've got one minute," one of the other team members told her sternly. "And then we're moving on."

Rox sank down on a rock and buried her face in her hands. This whole week had turned out to be a disaster, a totally worthless venture. She wasn't any closer to getting back with Vince than she'd been a week ago.

One of her teammates approached her. "We're going to take this route," he said, showing her on the map.

Roxanne didn't even bother to look. "I don't care," she said listlessly.

The guy gave her a look of disgust and went back to join the others. Rox sat there alone, dismally contemplating her fate.

And then she heard, very faintly, a familiar

voice coming from the thicket behind her. She peered through the bushes.

It was Vince and his team. They couldn't be more than ten yards away. The mere sound of his voice made her heart beat faster. She couldn't stand this any longer. She had to make contact with him and force him to look at her, listen to her and realize he still loved her. Tomorrow they'd be going back to Rose Hill, and she might not even see him again until school started. This was her last chance to get to him.

Suddenly she had an idea.

She hurried over to her teammates. "Look," she said to the heavy-set boy. "I don't think we should go that way." She indicated the direction she had heard Vince's voice. "I want to go this way."

They looked at each other and shook their heads in unison. "That's crazy," one of them said. "If we go that way, we'll have to go around that fence. It will end up taking us twice as long."

"I don't care if it does," Rox insisted. "I want to go that way."

"Why?" one of the others asked.

"Because . . . because I have a feeling it's the right way, that's all. Anyway, that's the way I'm going. And if you guys won't go with me, I'll go by myself."

"That's against the rules," a girl exclaimed. "We're supposed to stay together."

"I'm going that way," Rox said stubbornly. "You guys can do what you want." She knew they wouldn't insist she stay with them. They were all sick of listening to her complain.

122

Sure enough, the heavy-set boy shrugged. "You do what you want," he said. "We're going this way."

"That's fine with me," Rox shot back. And she headed off in the opposite direction.

Lin looked up from the compass. "Where'd the others go?" she asked Daniel.

"They went to check out that path," Daniel told her, showing her on the map.

"That's no good," Lin said. "It runs straight into that gulley. Why did they go there?"

"Because I told them to."

She looked at him curiously. "Why did you tell them to do that?"

"Because I wanted to be alone with you." His voice was husky.

Lin didn't look alarmed. Her gaze was steady and direct. And then it all just seemed to happen naturally. He held out his arms, and she folded into them. It was as if they were meant to be together like this. It was magic; it was like fireworks on the Fourth of July. Having her in his arms was better than anything he could have ever imagined.

Daniel had a feeling that he'd been searching for this girl all his life, a girl he didn't even know existed. He couldn't believe his good fortune in finding her. And as he held her tightly, he knew he'd never, ever let her go.

They kissed for what seemed like an eternity, but it was over much too quickly.

"I'm crazy about you," Daniel whispered.

When she didn't respond immediately, he held her tighter. "Lin?"

Her voice was muffled, but he didn't miss a word. "I'm crazy about you, too."

His heart soared. She cared for him, too! For the next few moments, they stood there, frozen, clinging together. Then Lin broke free.

"Why did you do that?" Daniel asked, alarmed.

Lin shook her head. "It's . . . it's happening too fast. We have to take it slower."

"Why?"

"Because that's the way I am." Her eyes implored him to understand. "I don't like to get into things too fast, Daniel."

"But you do care for me, don't you?"

Her eyes were soft. "Isn't that obvious?"

"Then why hold back?" Daniel asked urgently. "We both feel the same way. It's right, I can feel it."

"I'm sorry," Lin said simply. "It's the way I am."

For a moment, she stared at the ground. Then, almost unwillingly, she looked up. Their eyes locked. Almost reluctantly, as if it were against her will, she opened her arms to him.

And then they were holding each other again, as tightly as they could.

Roxanne moved slowly, trying to avoid the thorny bushes on both sides. To her right, she could faintly hear the voices of Vince and his teammates. The bushy thicket separated them, and they weren't aware yet that she was following them. She wanted to keep it that way, at least for a while. If she confronted him right now, he'd only be annoyed or embarrassed. She had to be patient, take her time, and wait for the right moment. She had a plan, but she had to find the circumstances that would enable her to put her plan into action.

The circumstances came about even sooner than she had expected. In front of her, she could see the edge of a steep gully. It wouldn't take much effort to get around it, but Rox had no intention of even trying.

She could hear the voices of Vince and his group right nearby. The timing was perfect. She sat down on the ground at the edge of the ridge. Slowly she allowed herself to slide down. At the same time, she let out a terrified scream.

Vince had just reached a small clearing in the thicket when he heard the scream. He recognized the voice immediately. He'd heard those cries for help before.

Peering through the clearing, he saw exactly what he expected to see. It was Roxanne, at the bottom of the gully, looking pitiful but unhurt. It was a clever stunt, he thought, but she'd pulled it once too often. He knew she expected him to come running and rescue her. And for a minute, he felt a tug on his heart. Using all his will power, he fought to ignore it.

He turned away so he couldn't see her. There was another cry, and this time it sounded desperate. But Vince had learned his lesson. He wasn't about to fall for one of Roxanne's ploys again.

"Did you hear that scream?" one of his teammates asked. "I think someone's in trouble."

"It's nothing," Vince assured him. "Someone tripped, that's all."

His teammates didn't look convinced. "Are you sure?"

Embarrassed, Vince explained. "It's Roxanne. We used to, uh, see each other. We broke up just a few weeks before camp. She's been trying to get my attention all week. This is just another of her tricks. She's pretending she's in trouble so I'll come running. Remember our big scene in the dining hall that day? Just ignore her."

His teammates had had enough experiences with Roxanne that week to believe him. Resolutely, Vince marched on, and the others followed.

A few seconds later, he heard another cry. This time it came from behind him. A second after that, he heard his own name being called, very faintly.

It sounded different this time. Vince stopped. The tug on his heart he'd felt earlier came back, and this time it was stronger than ever. There was an urgency in Roxanne's voice he hadn't heard earlier. Or maybe it was just his imagination.

He heard the cry again. Was that real pain he was hearing? Was it honest panic?

"Come on, Vince," one of his teammates urged.

Still, he couldn't move. She sounded so frightened, so desperate. "Wait a second," he told the others, and strained to hear the voice again.

The others gathered around him. "It's just that

126

Roxanne again," one of them said. "Like you said, she's just trying to get your attention."

The cries were fainter now, but Vince could still hear them. He hesitated. "I don't know," he said. "Maybe something's really wrong."

One of the guys looked at him skeptically. "Aw, come on, Vince, you told us she's an expert at this kind of thing. Don't fall for it again."

"Yeah," another group member echoed. "We're almost there. Don't let us down. If we don't all get there together, we can't win."

Vince just stood there. Once more, he heard the cry. Then his heart hardened. The memories flooded back, like a tape running fast-forward. Her cries outside the courtyard at school; her cries as she stood next to the wrecked car; her cries at his family's picnic — all those cries were turned on and off at will, and all were designed to make him fall for her. And, in the end, to make him look like a fool.

She's not going to do it to me again, he told himself fiercely. I've learned my lesson, finally. Roxanne Easton is crying wolf. And this time, for once, Vince DiMase isn't going to fall for it.

"Let's go," he said to the others harshly. And with a firm step, he left the false cries for help behind.

"Look!" Charlotte said excitedly, "It's just through there!"

Her teammates gathered around her. Sure enough, just through the break in the thicket, they could see the sign proclaiming PINE LAKE

CAMPGROUNDS AND CONFERENCE CENTER. They had reached their destination.

They pushed their way through the bushes and headed toward the sign. They weren't the first to get there. Charlotte saw Daniel, Lin, and the two boys gathered near Bob and Sharon. But her group was the second to come in, and that wasn't bad at all. Bob and Sharon congratulated them, and they hung around, waiting for the rest of the kids.

They didn't have to wait long. Vince and his team came in a few minutes later. Soon after that another group came in, and then another. Within minutes, all the groups had gathered around the sign.

They stood around, talking and comparing routes while Bob called the roll to make sure everyone was back.

"Group six," he bellowed. He called out the individual names. Each name was followed by a "here" until he reached Roxanne. There was a silence.

"Roxanne Easton," he called again. There was no reply.

Charlotte looked around. Roxanne was no-where to be seen.

"She's not here!" she cried out in alarm.

Bob turned to the team Roxanne had left with. "Where is she?"

Roxanne's team members looked distinctly un-comfortable. Finally, one of them spoke up.

"She wanted to go off in a different direction," he said. "So we let her."

Bob glared at them grimly. "You let her go off by herself? Even though you knew it was against the rules!"

"She refused to go along with the rest of us," the boy said defensively. "There was nothing we could do!"

Charlotte felt sick. She looked back at the dense, dark woods from which they'd all just emerged. Roxanne was in there, somewhere, all alone. She could be lost, or hurt.

Behind her Charlotte heard a gasp. She turned to see a white-faced Vince. For a brief second, her concern for Roxanne was replaced by the small satisfaction of realizing Vince must still care. Otherwise he wouldn't look so worried.

Their eyes met. "I heard her," Vince said softly.

"What?"

"I heard Roxanne call for help," Vince said miserably. "But I thought it was just another one of her tricks. I didn't even try to help her."

Charlotte was aghast. "Vince! How *could* you? She might be hurt!"

"I know," Vince moaned. He looked like he was on the verge of breaking down. Then he seemed to pull himself together. Quickly he pushed his way through the crowd toward Bob.

Charlotte watched as he engaged in a conversation with the camp leaders. She figured he must be telling them where he'd heard her cries for help.

Within seconds, Bob had the groups organized. They all went off in assigned directions to search for Roxanne.

It didn't take long. Charlotte's group got to the gully first. There, at the bottom, they saw Roxanne.

"I'll get her," Charlotte told the others. Quickly, she made her way down the slope. She recognized a patch of poison ivy and managed to avoid it. Deftly she climbed over some rocks and finally reached Roxanne.

Rox was sitting in the middle of a shallow stream.

"Are you okay?" Charlotte cried anxiously.

Roxanne turned slightly, and Charlotte could see real pain on her face.

"It's my ankle," Rox groaned. "I think it's probably broken."

Charlotte peered down at the ankle. "It doesn't look broken," she said. "There's no bruise or swelling. Maybe you just sprained it. See if you can stand up. Here, lean on me."

Rox struggled to her feet, managing to limp on her injured ankle. She rubbed her muddy legs. "I itch all over!" she cried.

Just wait until the morning, Charlotte thought, but she didn't tell her that. "C'mon, honey, I'll help you get back to the cabin."

"I don't want to go back to the cabin," Rox sobbed. "I want to go home."

"We're going home tomorrow," Charlotte reminded her.

"I don't want to go home tomorrow," Rox practically screamed. "I want to go home right now!"

By now, Bob and the others had reached the gully. They managed to pull Roxanne up the slope. Once they reached the top, Rox was calmer, but Charlotte could tell from her face that she was absolutely mortified.

"I want to go home," she kept saying. "I want to go back to Rose Hill."

Charlotte heard Sharon tell Bob she would call Mrs. Easton to drive Roxanne home. "We'll have the camp nurse take a look at that ankle," she said to Rox. "But you should probably have your mother take you to get it x-rayed, too, okay?"

"My mother!" Roxanne shook her head. "She's probably out having her nails done!"

"Well, someone ought to go with her," Bob said worriedly. "One of her friends. Someone who can take her to a doctor back in Rose Hill."

Inwardly Charlotte sighed. She hated to miss the big assembly that evening, and the last-night celebration that would undoubtedly follow. But Bob was right. Roxanne was in no condition to go home alone. And again, Charlotte felt a twinge of guilt. It was actually her fault that Roxanne had come to leadership camp in the first place.

"I'll go with her," she volunteered. She put her arm around Roxanne's shoulder.

"Come on, Rox," she said softly. "We're going home."

Chapter
13

The next morning Daniel woke up with a smile on his face. He hadn't slept much, but he felt great. Who needed sleep when you were in love?

He could hear the shower running in the bathroom, and he was glad not to have to make conversation with Vince for a few minutes. He wanted to be alone with his thoughts.

The camp party the night before had gone on till way past midnight. The whole group may have only been together one week, but the fact that they had been living, eating, and working together every day had made them a close-knit bunch. After all, a week was long enough to build up a lot of memories. And last night . . . last night was the best. Daniel closed his eyes slightly and tried to relive it in his mind.

When he first arrived at the party, he had scanned the room, trying to find Lin. Finally he saw her, or at least, he caught a brief glimpse of her. She was surrounded by a group of kids. He started to make his way over there, but he was stopped by a couple of guys who'd been in one of his role-playing groups.

"Hey, Tackett," one of them said, "you know, I almost punched you out the other day." The broad grin on the guy's face kept this from sounding like an actual threat.

"Oh, yeah?" Daniel raised his eyebrows. "How come?"

"It was that exercise yesterday," the boy explained. "You were doing a real head-honcho number, giving orders left and right."

"Yeah," the other boy agreed, "you were getting pretty bossy there, pushing everyone around. It was a good act, really convincing."

As Daniel recalled, it hadn't been an act. He'd just naturally taken charge. "I just wanted to get things going," he told them, tapping his foot impatiently. He wanted to get to Lin.

"That's what I figured," the boy said. "But you were coming on too strong! Maybe you could have been a little more . . . I don't know, uh — "

"Patient, maybe?" a feminine voice behind Daniel suggested.

Daniel turned, and immediately his face lit up. Lin was standing there with an amused expression on her face.

"Right, that's it," one of the boys stated. "You should be more patient."

Daniel wasn't even listening anymore. "Yeah, okay," he muttered. He couldn't take his eyes off Lin. There she was, in plain old jeans and a

T-shirt, just like any other girl there, and yet to him she stood out like a single star in a cloudless sky.

Her eyes were twinkling. "I see you haven't learned to be patient yet. Maybe you need some lessons."

Daniel grinned. "I wouldn't mind taking lessons — if you'll be my teacher."

Lin laughed out loud, a laugh that sounded like a thousand ringing bells. "That sounds good to me. I always did like a challenge."

"Here come the pizzas!" someone yelled.

Big cardboard boxes were being laid out on the tables. At first, Daniel thought he was too love-struck to think about food. But as more pizza boxes were opened, the aroma became irresistible. Daniel and Lin headed over to a table, and Daniel reached out to grab a slice.

"Ouch!" He pulled his hand back and sucked on his fingers. "They must have pulled this right out of the oven!"

Lin cocked her head to one side and smiled knowingly. "Lesson number one: If you're not patient, you could get burned."

Daniel grinned back at her. "Learning how to be patient isn't going to be easy."

Lin eyed him thoughtfully. "Nothing worth-while ever is."

Someone had brought a tape deck and cassettes, and later that evening the kids pushed back the tables and chairs in the dining hall and danced. At first, all the songs were fast ones. The campers were giddy, overtired from their week of intense work, and they all needed to let off steam. Daniel danced every song with Lin. For someone so reserved, she could really move. In fact, she was totally unselfconscious.

Maybe that was the reason he found her so fascinating. She was a complete paradox; totally unpredictable. And he liked the way she stood up to him.

He thought about the conversation he'd had earlier with the two boys. They were right. Daniel had a tendency to order people around. But he knew he'd never be able to push Lin around. She was as strong as he was.

There was so much about her that excited him. Her looks, of course, but so much more. There was her personality, her unique outlook, her intellect — everything about her was special.

Finally, a slow song came on the tape player. Dancing with his arms around her, Daniel had the oddest sensation. It was as if they were totally synchronized, and not just in their movements. He felt like their bodies, hearts, minds, even their souls, were in total harmony.

And he made a decision.

He wasn't going to let her drift out of his life. Leadership camp might be almost over, but he was determined not to let Lin become just another memory.

Reluctantly he forced himself to come back to the present. He jumped out of bed, dressed, and began to pack his clothes. The bus would be leaving soon after breakfast, and he wanted to make sure he and Lin got seats together. There were all kinds of plans and arrangements to make. He had to get her address and phone number in D.C., and then figure out when they could meet.

Vince emerged from the bathroom with a towel wrapped around him. His "good morning" was lethargic, and Daniel couldn't help noticing he could barely keep his eyes open. Obviously, Vince hadn't slept well the night before, either, but it couldn't have been because of the party. He'd only stayed there for a brief time before telling Daniel he was tired and going back to the cabin. When Daniel returned, though, Vince wasn't in his bed.

"Where'd you go off to last night?" Daniel asked him. He wasn't really all that interested, but he felt like he had to make sure Vince was okay.

"Took a walk," Vince said. "I wasn't feeling too great."

Daniel tried to look sympathetic. "Roxanne?"

"Yeah." Vince started tossing things into his pack. "I felt like a real jerk. I heard her calling for help, and I just ignored her. Now everyone — including Bob and Sharon — thinks I'm a real creep for not trying to rescue her."

"It was probably just another one of her little games," Daniel said. "I'm sure she slid down the slope on purpose. She just didn't plan on getting hurt and not being able to get back up."

Vince nodded. "I know that. Still, I should have helped her." He sighed deeply. "On one hand, I feel bad about that. But on the other hand, she made me feel like a jerk again."

Daniel didn't know what else to say. "Well, that's the kind of girl she is." He tried to imagine himself falling for a girl like that. Impossible. He'd known her too long and too well. Then he tried to picture Lin making him feel like a jerk. No way.

Suddenly, Daniel remembered that he was wasting precious time he could be spending with Lin. "Look, I want to go grab some breakfast before we leave. See you on the bus."

Grabbing his duffel bag, he dashed out the door and headed toward the dining hall. When he got there, he saw that the bus had already arrived. It was parked in front of the building. With some alarm, he noticed a couple of kids inside it, throwing their bags on seats to reserve them.

He decided to find Lin right away, get her bag, and make a claim on two seats — preferably seats in the back.

He saw her in the dining hall, and his heart sank a little when he realized she was engrossed in a conversation with Bob and Sharon. Well, they'd have time to make their plans during the bus ride.

He ran over to the table where they were sitting. "Sorry to interrupt," he said hastily, then turned to Lin. "Where's your suitcase?"

Lin raised her eyebrows. "Why do you want to know where my suitcase is?"

"Because I need to put it on the bus with mine. I want to make sure we get to sit together."

Lin smiled slightly, but it wasn't a happy smile. "On, Daniel, I'm sorry. I'm not taking the bus."

Daniel started at her stupidly. "You're not taking the bus?" he repeated.

Lin shook her head. "My parents are picking me up here. I'm going to look at colleges."

"But I need to talk to you," Daniel said

urgently. Suddenly he felt panic-stricken, as if she were going to get into her parents' car and ride out of his life forever.

Lin started to indicate the empty chair at the table, but something in his eyes must have told her he had to see her alone. "Excuse me," she said politely to Bob and Sharon. She got up and turned to Daniel. "Let's go for a walk. But I have to be right back. My parents should be here in twenty minutes, and they're always right on time."

All thoughts of breakfast had vanished. Only twenty minutes! He hurried Lin out of the dining hall, and automatically they walked to their special place — the log by the creek.

He couldn't decide whether they should kiss first or talk first. He decided that if he started kissing her, he might not be able to stop.

Taking a deep breath, he said, "Lin, I guess you must know by now how I feel about you." He paused briefly to make sure she was nodding, but he didn't give her any time to respond. "This wasn't just a one-week fling, at least not for me. I've never felt like this about any other girl before, ever; I swear it. I'm crazy about you."

Lin's eyes were soft, and she was smiling. Encouraged, Daniel continued. "I want to see you again, as soon as possible, right away. You don't live that far from me, you know. And I've got a car."

Her smile began to fade. The happiness on her face was slowly replaced by something else, some expression Daniel couldn't identify. Suddenly, he became apprehensive, and he started talking even faster.

"How about this weekend? Friday night . . . or Saturday night . . . or how about both? I could pick you up, and we'll go out to dinner in D.C., and then maybe we could go to a movie, or a play, or just take a walk, whatever you want."

He could hear himself babbling, but he couldn't stop.

"Look, I know you think I'm impatient, and maybe you're right, but so what? I know you feel the same way about me." When she didn't say anything right away, all his confidence evaporated. "Don't you?"

Slowly, Lin nodded, and he felt waves of relief rush over him.

"Yes," she said softly. "I do feel the same way about you. Maybe I don't show my feelings as easily as you do, but they're there, and they're just as strong."

Daniel wanted to grab her right then and there, but there were still plans to be made. "Then I'll call you tonight, okay? What's your number?"

For a moment, Lin was silent. Then she shook her head. "You mustn't call me, Daniel. Not yet."

Daniel was bewildered. "Why not?"

Lin picked up a pebble and tossed it into the creek. "Daniel, listen to me. I do care for you, so much. But we can't get together right away. When the time is right, I'll call you, I promise you that. Until then, you'll just have to be patient. Can you do that?" She reached up and gently touched his cheek. "Try to understand."

He couldn't. All he knew was that he wanted to be with this girl, this wonderful, enchanting girl, forever and ever. He put his hand over hers. Then they kissed.

Lin pulled back. "I must go," she said. "My parents will be here. Remember, Daniel, you mustn't call! You'll be hearing from me soon, I promise." She blew him a kiss. And then she was gone.

For a second, Daniel just sat there, dazed. What had she meant? Why couldn't he call her? What was so important about being patient? Then he got up and ran after her.

When he reached the parking lot in front of the dining hall, he saw her getting into the back-seat of a car. Frantically, he called out, "Lin!" and waved his arms. Slowly, her face turned toward him. Even from that distance, he could see the longing in her expression as their eyes met.

But she didn't smile or wave. Then the car glided out of the lot, and she was gone.

Chapter
14

K atie stuck her head into the kitchen, where her parents were sitting drinking coffee.

"I'm going over to Karen's now," she told them.

"Isn't Greg coming to pick you up?" her mother asked.

Katie hesitated. She hadn't told her mother about their fight, and she didn't feel like getting into it now. "He's meeting me there later."

"You don't want to stay out too late," her father cautioned her. "We've got a long trip tomorrow." Her father was driving her down to school, and the car was already packed. Tonight was her farewell party. Too bad she wasn't in much of a party mood.

"I won't," she promised. Her parents were looking at her a little sadly, as if they missed her already. She forced herself to smile for them. Stepping into the room, she struck a pose.

"How do I look?"

"Very nice," her mother commented.

"Gorgeous," her father added, with his usual tendency to exaggerate.

Her brothers wolf-whistled in unison.

But she *did* look nice — she knew that. Katie was glad she hadn't already packed her favorite green linen pants. She was wearing them with a pale yellow silk T-shirt and little gold flats. She'd also chosen large gold hoop earrings and a thin gold chain to go around her neck. Her freshly washed hair gleamed, and she'd even found time to give herself a manicure.

Katie'd dressed with extra care that night, and not just because the party was in her honor. She was thinking about Greg. She hadn't heard from him at all since their argument at the mall, but she knew he'd be there. And it would be the last time she'd see him until Christmas.

What would it be like when she saw him? she wondered as she slowly walked to Karen's. She was feeling confused, and she still couldn't quite figure out what had happened between them, why they were both so angry. It wasn't just that she had felt pressured, harried, and tired of running around. It was more than that. There was something they weren't saying to each other, something neither of them could admit.

For her part, she knew what it was. She was scared. It was that simple. And it wasn't just the fear of the unknown, of what life at college would be like. She was apprehensive about that, of course. But she was more fearful of what the separation would mean for her and Greg.

For so long he'd been a major part of her life.

And now he wouldn't be. She'd tried to talk to him about it, but he wouldn't listen. A horrible thought struck her. Maybe he just didn't care. Maybe their impending separation didn't frighten him the way it frightened her.

That's why he'd planned so many activities this last week, Katie reasoned. He saw it as a last fling, the finale of their relationship. The same thing had happened with his previous girlfriend, Chris. Once she left for college, it was all over between them. By next week, Greg would have forgotten all about her. He'd be looking around for another girl to hang out with, to take to football games and parties. And Katie would be nothing more than a pleasant memory.

By the time she reached Karen's house, she was thoroughly depressed. Standing on the doorstep pushing the buzzer, she prepared herself for the question she knew she would hear from whoever opened the door.

It was Karen, looking elegant in a blue poplin jumpsuit. "Hey, it's the guest of honor," she called over her shoulder, then turned back and beamed at Katie. "Welcome! Where's Greg?"

Katie made a supreme effort to look happy. "He'll be coming soon. Hey, I love what you're wearing!"

Inside the house, the party was already in full swing. All her friends were there, and the mood was up. They'd all gathered to wish her farewell, and Katie wanted to show them how much she appreciated it. But already the strain of forcing a smile was making her jaws ache.

Even through her gloom, Katie could tell that

Karen and Brian had really knocked themselves out. A huge sign proclaimed in glittery letters WE'LL MISS YOU, KATIE! Crepe-paper streamers were strung from wall to wall, and above their heads, helium ballons bobbed on the ceiling.

"Karen, this is wonderful!" Katie exclaimed. "It looks like, like — "

"I know," Karen interrupted, laughing. "It looks like a little kid's birthday party. Brian and I had a big discussion about it. First we were going to make it very sophisticated, with hors d'oeuvres and formal dress or something. You know, here we are, all going off to college, we ought to have an 'adult' party. But then Brian said, let's have one last shot at being jerky kids again. Let's all just get silly and crazy and forget all that heavy stuff for an evening."

Katie wished she could. She managed to give Karen a big appreciative hug anyway, saying, "I love it!" Even as she spoke, she had a feeling she didn't sound terribly convincing.

Karen eyed her suspiciously. "Something's obviously wrong."

Katie sighed. "Oh, Karen, I'm just going to miss you all so much."

Karen gave her a quick hug. "And we're going to miss you, too. We're all going to be missing each other." She looked around the room and smiled wistfully. "It's hard to believe we're all splitting up."

Katie agreed. "We've had some great times."

Brian joined them in time to hear those last words. "And we'll have more great times," he said firmly. "After all, we'll be back together on vacations."

"That's right," Katie murmured. But somehow she had trouble visualizing any more great times without Greg.

Making her way through the crowd, she paused when she saw Daniel. He was sitting alone, staring at nothing, and his eyes had a funny, glazed look.

"How was leadership camp?" she asked him.

He stared at her blankly for a second. Then he grinned. "Incredible. Fabulous."

"Really? What happened?"

"I fell in love."

"Oh, that's really nice. Congratulations." Katie tried to sound happy for him, but she didn't want to hear any more. Tonight she just didn't want to hear about the joys of being in love. It was something she didn't want to think about.

"Hi, Katie," Jonathan greeted her, his arm loosely draped around Lily's shoulder. "Great party, huh?"

Katie nodded. "Really great." She was having a hard time looking at the happy couple in front of her. They were so much in love.

"I'm going to give a party next month when Jonathan and the other seniors leave for college," Lily told her.

"That's nice," Katie said wistfully. It was hard to picture a party with her not being there. She wondered who Greg would go with.

She went out to the terrace, where a bunch of kids were gathered around the grill, flipping hamburgers.

"Hey, Katie!" Charlotte DeVries called out merrily. "Where's Greg?"

Katie eyed her suspiciously. She liked her, but Charlotte was a major flirt. Greg could easily fall prey to her friendly, outgoing nature.

"I don't know," she said abruptly, and then regretted her tone. She had no reason to dislike Charlotte. Katie made an effort to sound friendlier. "How was leadership camp?"

"It was great," Charlotte bubbled. "I had to leave early, though, because of Roxanne."

Hearing that name made Katie flinch. Roxanne had gone after Greg several times. Was *she* planning to make another stab at winning his affections? "What happened to Roxanne?"

She was barely listening as Charlotte went into a long, involved description about what happened to Roxanne at leadership camp. Her ears were straining to hear the sound of the doorbell. Where *was* Greg, anyway?

She caught the tail end of Charlotte's story, something about Roxanne falling down a gully. "That's too bad," she murmured. "Uh, I'm going to get something to eat."

She wasn't really hungry at all. She was just looking for an excuse to keep moving.

Matt Jacobs was handling the grill. "Hey, Katie, how do you like your hamburger?"

"Later," Katie called back to him. She wandered over to the other side of the deck. A table was laden with salads and munchies and a big fruit bowl. She joined Molly Ramirez, who was busy filling her plate.

"Hi, K.C.!" Molly greeted her. Then she caught

146

Katie's expression, and her smile faded. "Okay, what's wrong? Do you miss us all already?"

Katie couldn't put up a cheery act for Molly. Her best friend would see right through it.

Molly listened sympathetically as Katie told her about the events of the past week. "You must have been exhausted," she said. "But don't be too hard on Greg. He was just trying to show you a good time."

"Sure," Katie said bitterly, "so he wouldn't have to feel guilty about finding a new girlfriend the second I leave town."

"You don't know that's true," Molly told her sternly.

"Why else would he be running me around like that?" Katie asked. "Every time I tried to talk about *us*, he wouldn't even listen."

"You don't know what's going on in his head. Talk to him tonight," Molly urged. "Don't leave with bad feelings."

"I'll try," Katie promised. But she knew her voice lacked conviction.

She wandered back inside. Someone had turned up the music, and kids were headed downstairs to dance. "Katie, come on, let's tear up the dance floor," Brian called to her.

"I'll be down in a second," Katie replied. But instead of following him, she went to the window and peered out.

She couldn't believe what she saw. Greg's mom's white Mercedes was parked right in front, and she could see him sitting inside.

How long had he been there? She watched him sitting there, motionless. Finally, he got out of the car and came toward the house. And as she watched him approach, she felt a rush of love for him. They had to talk.

Greg stood on the doorstep, but he didn't press the bell right away. He was still thinking about what he wanted to say to Katie.

He couldn't let it end this way. She was too important to him. He had to confess the truth to her. He had to let her know why he'd been acting like such a fool.

He aimed a finger at the bell, but before he could hit it, the door flew open. And there she was.

"Hi," she said softly.

"Hi," he replied.

They stood there for a moment, just looking at each other. There was so much he wanted to tell her, but at that moment, he almost felt as if no words were necessary. Surely she could read what he was feeling in his eyes.

But maybe not. Katie's face was expressionless.

"We have to talk," he said gruffly.

Silently, Katie nodded and opened the door wider. He went inside and looked around the empty room. "Where is everyone?"

"Downstairs, dancing."

Now he could hear the pulsating beat of the music coming from the basement. He stood there awkwardly, unsure of how to begin.

"Let's go outside," Katie said. He followed her out onto the terrace.

Once they were outside, they both started talking at once.

"Greg, I have to say — "

"Katie, I want to tell you — "

They both stopped and laughed nervously.

"You go first," Katie said.

Greg took a deep breath. "I know I've been acting like a crazy person all week. I just couldn't face the fact that you were leaving. I couldn't cope with it. I, uh, I made up that schedule so we'd be busy all the time, so I'd have no time to think about saying good-bye." His voice cracked, and he looked away. "Oh, Katie, I'm going to miss you so much."

When he looked back at her, he saw a tear edging its way down her cheek. "Greg, I can't tell you how much I'm going to miss you. I get so scared just thinking about it. That's why I was so tense, so out of it."

"I'm sorry I was such a jerk," Greg told her. "I should have realized you'd need some time alone. And when you tried to tell me that, I wouldn't listen to you."

Katie shook her head. "I'm the one who should apologize. You've always been so good to me. When I broke my leg and practically blamed you for it, you never gave up on me. You helped me get into the U of Florida. And you gave up going to leadership camp for me."

"I did that for me, too," Greg said. "I knew I'd rather be with you than at camp."

Katie looked at him ruefully. "And I never even said thank you."

Greg grinned. "I never gave you time to say thank you." He took her hand. They stood on the edge of the terrace and looked out over the yard.

"We've both been pretty silly," Katie said. "We've spent the last two days not even speaking to each other. What a waste of time."

"Maybe not," Greg said. "Maybe we both needed that time alone."

Katie looked up. "Look," she whispered. "It's a full moon. And there's the first star." She closed her eyes. " 'Star light, star bright, first star I see tonight. I wish I may, I wish I might, have the wish I wish tonight.' " Then she opened her eyes and gazed steadily at Greg. "I don't know what to wish for."

Greg did. He knew what he wanted, more than anything else. "Wish for us. Wish that tonight could go on forever."

For a moment, she was silent. "But it can't, Greg," she said finally, regretfully. "I'm leaving tomorrow. And we need to talk about what's going to happen to us."

"What do you want to happen?" Greg asked.

Katie didn't even have to think before answering. "I want to go on loving you, forever and always. And I want you to go on loving me."

"Forever and always," Greg echoed.

She paused, unwilling to say what Greg knew she had to say.

"But . . ." he prompted her.

"But we can't predict the future. Who knows what will happen to us this next year. Who knows what we'll do, where we'll go, or. . . ."

"Who we'll meet," Greg finished.

Katie nodded sadly.

"I think," Greg said slowly, "we'll just have to wait and see. We have to take each day, each experience, as it comes. And whatever happens, we'll deal with it."

"I'll never stop loving you," Katie said.

Greg smiled at her tenderly. "And I'll never stop loving you." Now came the hardest thing he had to say. But he felt that now, finally, he had the strength to say it. He took her hands.

"But Katie, people change. When you're down in Florida, I don't want you to feel bound by some commitment to me. I want you to feel free to be open to new experiences and . . . and new people. I only want you to promise me one thing. . . ."

"What's that?"

"Talk to me. Let me know what's going on. And don't ever be afraid to tell me the truth. Even if you think it will hurt me."

He could feel a heavy ache in his heart as he said this. He would rather have said, "Be true to me, Katie. Don't ever love anyone else." But it wouldn't have been fair. Not to her, and not to him.

"All right," Katie said. "But you have to promise the same to me."

"You've got it," Greg replied. He took her in his arms, and they kissed for a long time. And when they finally stopped kissing, they just stood there, holding each other. And even though he would soon have to let her go, Greg knew that in his heart he'd go on holding her like this, forever and always.

Chapter
15

A week later, Charlotte was getting ready to leave her house when the phone rang. "Hello?"

"Hi, it's me. What are you doing?"

"Hi, Rox," Charlotte said. "I was just on my way to school."

"What are you going to school for?" Roxanne asked.

"Today's the last day for registration corrections," Charlotte told her. "I have to change something on my schedule. I want to try and get into a government class."

"I'm taking that," Rox said. "Try to get it third period, and we can be in the same class."

Charlotte made a note of that. "Okay. How are you feeling?"

"Much better. I don't itch anymore, and the rash is almost completely gone. My ankle's fine, too. By tomorrow I might actually be able to leave the house."

"Great," Charlotte said warmly.

"You know," Rox continued, "I've had a lot of time to think this past week, just lying in bed. I decided I've been acting really foolish."

"How do you mean?"

"Oh, trying to get Vince back. Pretending to get burned, falling into that gully — I was so stupid to think I could get his attention that way." Her voice was sad, but firm. "I can't get him back, Charlotte. I have to give up."

"Do you still care about him?" Charlotte asked.

"I'll never stop caring about him," Rox admitted. "But I have to accept the fact that I can't force him to love me, no matter what kind of stunt I pull."

"Maybe you're right," Charlotte said. "But you never know what can happen. He might come around eventually."

"Maybe," Rox murmured. But her tone didn't carry much hope.

Charlotte's heart went out to her. In the past week, she'd become closer to Roxanne. She'd talked with her on the phone every day and visited her at home. Rox might have gotten on her nerves a bit at camp, but now Charlotte felt as if she was beginning to understand her better. When she wasn't whining and complaining, Rox was a different person.

Seeing Rox at home had made Charlotte much more aware of where her friend was coming from. There, in the fancy, formal town house, she'd seen Roxanne's loneliness and the absence of love in her life. She'd met Rox's jet-set mother, who didn't seem to have any interest at all in her daughter. And she'd gotten a glimpse of Torrey, Rox's sulky brother, who struck Charlotte as wild and irresponsible — definitely not someone who could ever be supportive to Rox.

Charlotte had always had a soft spot in her heart for anyone in need, and Roxanne needed a friend, someone who wouldn't let her down.

"Listen," she said, "how about if I drop by after I finish this registration business at school?"

She was pleased to hear Rox's tone lift. "Really? That would be great."

"I'll see you later," Charlotte promised.

Vince stood in the school entranceway and studied his schedule. He had to change his math section. Last June he'd requested that section specifically because Roxanne was in it. Now he wanted out. He couldn't deal with the thought of sitting in the same room with her day after day. There was no telling what she might pull.

He was still feeling uncomfortable about what had happened at leadership camp, too. The day he returned, he was too embarrassed to go to Karen's party for Katie. Everyone would have probably heard about it by then. He envisioned them all looking at him in scorn and thinking, Some rescue squad hero — he couldn't even save poor, pathetic Roxanne.

But during the past week, he'd run into several kids from the crowd, and no one seemed to know what had happened. He felt relieved that his reputation wasn't completely shot.

But he still had mixed feelings about Roxanne. He remembered that moment when he saw her lying at the bottom of the gully. For a second, he had thought she might be seriously hurt, and a shot of real fear had flashed through him. But he wasn't sure if that was because he still cared for her, or if he just felt guilty for not coming to her rescue when she called for help.

He wondered how she was doing. She'd really taken a bath in that poison ivy, and from personal experience Vince knew how unpleasant that could be. He probably should have called her this week, just to see how she was feeling.

But he couldn't bring himself to do that. He was afraid any gesture on his part might make matters worse. It just wouldn't be a wise move.

Trying to shake off his guilt, he went into the guidance office and approached the counselor. "I'd like to change this math course to another section," he told her, handing her his forms.

The counselor looked the forms over. "I don't see any conflict here with another course."

"I still want to switch it," Vince said.

The counselor frowned. "Why?"

"I just need to be in a different class," Vince said, feeling stupid.

The counselor pulled out another form and began filling it out. Then she stopped.

"You have to give me some sort of explanation," she said. "Why do you want to be in a different section?"

Vince looked at the form, and scratched his head. "How about just, uh, personal reasons?"

The counselor looked at him blankly. But then, to his relief, she simply shrugged and wrote that down.

There were several people waiting in front of the guidance office, and Charlotte took her place in line. She was studying her schedule when she heard a deep, masculine voice say, "Hi, Charlotte."

She looked up and smiled. "Hi, Vince. Are you getting your schedule changed?"

He nodded but didn't offer any further explanation. He just stood there, looking distinctly uncomfortable, as if there was something he wanted to say but he wasn't sure how to say it.

"Me, too," Charlotte said. "I want to get into that new government class. All the seniors said it was really interesting."

Again Vince just nodded. Then he blurted out, "How's Roxanne?"

Charlotte was a little startled by the abrupt question. She'd planned to avoid bringing up Roxanne's name the next time she saw Vince. She figured he wouldn't want to hear about her. But maybe she was wrong. Maybe Vince still felt something for Rox.

"She's better," Charlotte told him. "The poison ivy's almost completely gone."

"Good," Vince replied. He frowned, and then in a rush he asked, "Do you think she fell into that gully on purpose?"

Charlotte didn't know how to respond. To admit what she knew would be betraying her friend, but she was never any good at lying.

Her silence answered for her, and Vince shook his head sadly. "She's got to stop doing things like that. It's not going to do any good."

156

"She knows, Vince," Charlotte said gently. "She realizes how foolish she's been."

Vince looked at her hopefully. "Really?"

Charlotte nodded. "Rox is really a good person, Vince. She just wants to be loved, and she doesn't know anything about how to love in return. You know, most of us are lucky. We grew up with great, caring families. But Rox never had that. She's always felt she had to manipulate people into caring about her. I think now she's beginning to see that manipulating people only ends up getting you hurt. What she needs is friends."

Vince looked pensive, obviously trying to absorb what she had said. Charlotte watched him warily, preparing to defend Roxanne if he started attacking her.

To her surprise, Vince responded calmly and thoughtfully. "You're right," he said. "And she's lucky to have you as a friend. Thanks for helping her."

Listening to him, Charlotte realized that Roxanne was right — Vince wasn't going to come back to her. It was funny, Charlotte thought. If Vince had been steaming about Rox, she would have thought there still might be hope for them. When a person's really angry at someone, that means there are strong feelings there. But Vince sounded like he only wanted to be Roxanne's friend — and nothing more.

Suddenly she felt very, very sad for her friend. Roxanne was still in love with Vince, and for him, the relationship was completely and totally finished.

"You know," Vince continued, "I've been

feeling pretty guilty about not calling her. But I just didn't think it was wise, considering the past. I didn't want to lead her on and let her think there was still hope for us. I didn't want to hurt her anymore than she's already been hurt."

He's a good person, Charlotte thought. Even if he's not in love with Roxanne anymore, he still cares what happens to her. Even though she knew there was no hope for Rox, her opinion of Vince went way up.

"I'll try to make her understand," she said softly.

"Thanks." Vince's tone was gruff, but something in his eyes told her he really appreciated her help.

For a second, they just stood there looking at each other. Suddenly, Charlotte felt uneasy. "I, uh, better get going on this," she said. "It's my turn," she added lamely.

Vince gave her a half smile. "See you later."

Charlotte started to go into the office. But with her hand on the doorknob, she found herself turning to look back at him. To her surprise, Vince was still looking at her. Quickly he looked away, and so did she. And she realized her heart was pounding in a most peculiar way.

It was as if she had just seen him for the very first time. Why had she never realized before how attractive he was? And he was so nice, too, so gentle and caring and mature.

But that's not all he is, she thought. He's the ex-boyfriend of my new best friend, Charlotte reminded herself.

And with all the willpower she could muster,

she tried to push aside the new, disturbing feelings and went into the office.

Daniel parked his car in the Kennedy High parking lot, walked into the building, and headed for the guidance office. He groaned when he saw the line in front of the door. When Greg emerged from the office, Daniel called him over. At least he could pass a few minutes talking to Greg. And it might take his mind off something else.

But Greg didn't seem to be in the mood for conversation.

"What's up?" Daniel asked.

Greg shrugged. "Not much."

"Did Katie get off to Florida okay?"

Greg nodded silently.

If this conversation had taken place a month earlier, Daniel knew he wouldn't even have noticed Greg's mood. But now he knew what it was like to be separated from someone you cared about.

"It's rough, isn't it?" he remarked.

"Yeah," Greg replied glumly. "Hey, look, I'll see you later."

Daniel watched him trudge down the hall. Even his walk was a clear indication of how he was feeling. And Daniel could relate to it.

It had been a week since leadership camp had ended, and he still hadn't heard from Lin. The day he left camp, he had promised himself he'd be patient, just like she'd asked him to be. He had decided he'd give her one week to call him. Now the week was over, and he didn't know what to do.

He couldn't get her out of his mind. Every time

he closed his eyes, he saw her face — those dark eyes, the half smile, that long, flowing black hair. In his mind he could hear her voice and feel the thrill that had shot through him each time he saw her. He knew she felt the same way about him. Then why hadn't she called?

Give her time, he kept telling himself. Don't rush things. Think about something else.

It was his turn to go into the guidance office, and that provided a brief distraction.

"I need to have my schedule changed to include two journalism periods," he told the counselor. "I'm the new editor of *The Red and the Gold*," he added by way of explanation.

The counselor smiled at him. "Well, that's quite an honor," she said. "Congratulations."

It was funny, Daniel thought as the counselor made the adjustments to his form. Just weeks ago, those words would have made him stand up a little straighter. After all, becoming editor of the newspaper was what he had wanted more than anything else, and he'd knocked himself out to get the appointment. Just thinking about being editor had given him a rush of adrenaline. And when Karen had finally announced his appointment at the senior bonfire on the beach in June, he'd felt like he was on top of the world.

Where was the thrill now? He felt . . . nothing. Leaving the office, he felt like he was walking through a misty cloud of gloom that he was incapable of shaking off.

"Daniel!"

He turned to see Mr. Kulp, next term's newspaper advisor, coming toward him.

"Just the man I wanted to see," Mr. Kulp said jovially. "I've been expecting you to come by my office this week."

Daniel looked at him blankly, and then vaguely remembered that he was supposed to stop by to pick up some materials.

"Right," he said lamely, "I, uh, was just on my way to your office now."

"Well, you're headed in the wrong direction," the teacher remarked. "Come along. I've got a lot of stuff to give you."

Daniel followed him to his office. On Mr. Kulp's desk were five fat folders. "This is the information on advertising," he said, "and this one has all the statistics on production costs." As he piled the folders in Daniel's arms, he went on to describe the contents of each. Daniel was barely listening.

"Daniel!" the newspaper advisor said sharply. "Are you listening to me?"

"Yes, sir," Daniel said quickly, trying to focus his attention.

"I was telling you about the big statewide competition next year for high school newspapers. There's a very prestigious award at stake, and I think Kennedy has a good chance of winning it. But you need to come up with some really innovative ideas for the paper. We want *The Red and the Gold* to stand out and look like more than just another ordinary high school newspaper. It's not enough to have competent reporting. I think you should start going through these folders immediately and see if you can come up with some creative ideas."

When Daniel didn't say anything immediately,

Mr. Kulp frowned. "You don't seem very enthusiastic about this."

"Oh, I am, I am," Daniel assured him quickly. "I was just, uh, thinking." But not about the newspaper, he added silently. "I'll take these to the office right now and get started on them."

At least this should take his mind off Lin, he thought as he lugged the stack of folders to the newspaper office. He tossed them on the desk at the front of the room and sat down.

He fingered the small plaque on the desk that proclaimed him editor in chief. Well, there he was, right where he'd hoped and dreamed of being. Sitting at this desk had been his goal. He'd worked hard to get there, and he'd succeeded. Then why did he feel so empty?

He opened one of the folders and stared at the top sheet. But he couldn't read it. It was all just words and numbers, totally meaningless. All he could think about was Lin.

Maybe she'd changed her mind. Maybe he'd misinterpreted her feelings. Maybe she didn't care about him at all. Maybe she had a boyfriend in D.C. Maybe, maybe, maybe . . . he felt like he was going crazy with the doubts and the fears.

He couldn't take it any longer. He had to know what was going on. He grabbed the folders, stuck them in a drawer, and ran out of the room.

Chapter
16

Getting to D.C. was no problem. Fifteen minutes later, Daniel was within District limits. It wasn't until he arrived in the downtown area that something dawned on him — he didn't have the slightest idea where Lin lived. He knew it was somewhere downtown, but that was all.

For a few minutes he drove around aimlessly, unsure as to what his next step should be. Finally, he parked the car, got out, and started walking. Then he spotted a large building, and his pace quickened. It was a public library. As a reporter, he knew the value of libraries for getting information. Hurrying into the building, he located the reference department.

"I need a telephone book," he told the librarian breathlessly. "The white pages."

She gave him one, and he sat down at a table. He flipped through it until he reached the P's, and then he groaned out loud. Several people around him frowned, and one made a shushing sound. Daniel ignored them. He just stared at the page in dismay.

There must have been fifty Parks.

It was too much to hope that she might have her own phone. He checked anyway, but there wasn't any Lin listed among the Parks. And he had no idea what her father's first name was.

He leaned back and tried to think. You're a reporter, he told himself. You've done investigative work before. Just think clearly and logically, and you'll come up with a way to figure out which Park you want.

He thought back to the conversations he'd had with Lin at camp. He tried to remember if she'd said anything that might give him a clue: the name of a street, a landmark, a famous building. . . .

Suddenly, he sat upright. Her school! He distinctly remembered her saying something about walking to school. And he remembered the name of the school — sort of. It was Saint something.

He flipped through the pages of the phone directory to the S's. There were three high schools named for saints. Taking the book with him, he went to the pay phone by the entrance.

He dialed the first one. "Good afternoon, Saint Agnes Prep," said the voice that answered.

"Do you have a student registered there named Lin Park?" he asked in a rush.

"I'm sorry," the voice replied pleasantly. "We do not give out that information."

Daniel hung up and frowned. If that school wouldn't tell him, the others probably wouldn't either. He paused to think. Luckily, his investigative skills didn't fail him. He had another idea.

He went back to the librarian. "Do you have a street map of Washington?"

The librarian nodded and handed him a book with detailed maps of every section of the city. Daniel went back to the table with the phone book and the map and got down to work. He checked the addresses of the Saint schools and looked for them on the map.

Only one, Saint Catherine's, was in the downtown area. He located it and drew an imaginary circle around it, covering what he figured would be walking distance.

Then he went back to the list of Parks and slowly, laboriously, looked for each street address to see if it was within his circle. He identified five Parks that looked like they'd be within walking distance of Saint Catherine's. Jotting down the numbers, he went back to the phone.

By now his heart was pounding. When he realized he didn't have any more quarters, he almost exploded. He ran back to the reference desk.

"I need change for the phone," he said, thrusting a bill at the librarian.

"I'm sorry, we don't make change," the librarian said kindly. But Daniel wasn't about to accept that.

"Please, it's important," he pleaded. "It's, uh, an emergency!" Even as he said it, he couldn't believe he was talking like this to the librarian. Now she'd probably think he was some kind of troublemaker and throw him out.

But she must have read the urgency in Daniel's face. Her expression softened, and she relented. "Wait a minute," she whispered, "I think I've got some change." She rummaged under the desk and came up with four quarters.

"Thanks," Daniel said, and ran back to the phone. To his despair, someone else was using it.

"Hurry up, hurry up," he muttered, feeling more and more frantic with every passing minute. He knew he was being completely irrational. Why did he feel it was so vital that he reach Lin right this minute? Why did he have this fear that if he waited too long, he'd lose her?

Finally, the phone was free. He dialed the first Park. "Could I speak with Lin, please?"

"I'm sorry, you must have the wrong number," came the response. "There's no Lin here."

Muttering a hasty "Sorry," he hung up and tried the next one. There was no Lin at that number, either.

The third Park didn't answer. The fourth was another wrong number, and the fifth was busy. He could wait there a while and try the fifth one again, but he couldn't stand not doing something. He decided to take a chance and go there.

He checked the map again to see how to get to the home of the fifth Park. Then he ran out of the library and raced to his car.

He drove in circles for a while looking for the street, but finally he located it. Slowly, he drove down the street, peering at the house numbers. Then he saw it.

Of course, he still couldn't be sure it was the right Park. The right one might have been the one who didn't answer. But somehow, as he gazed at the pleasant, neat, modest house, he knew it had to be Lin's. An upstairs window was open, and he could see inside it there was a row of flowering plants. Was it Lin's room? Maybe he'd find out very soon.

The cars were parked bumper to bumper on the street, and he cruised up and down, looking for a parking place. Miraculously, a car pulled away right in front of the house that was maybe Lin's. It's a sign, he decided. This has to be the right place.

Carefully, he edged into the space. He didn't want to risk hitting the cars in front or back — one of them might be Lin's parents'. Then he jumped out of the car and ran up to the doorstep. Taking a deep breath, he hit the buzzer.

It was like a dream come true, maybe even a miracle.

Lin opened the door.

Just seeing her standing there took his breath away. He felt as if he'd momentarily lost her, and then found her again. Lin's mouth fell open in surprise, but Daniel didn't give her a chance to speak. He threw his arms around her and kissed her passionately.

For a moment, it was just as it had been at camp. Every love song he'd ever heard rang in his head. Fireworks exploded in his ears, waves crashed on a shore, stars appeared in the middle

167

of the afternoon sky and smiled down on them. The feelings were almost unbearable. He never knew such happiness existed.

Then, from behind her, he heard a gasp. Lin pushed him away, and he opened his eyes. Just behind her in the hallway stood her mother. And the older woman didn't look very pleased to see him there. In fact, she was staring at him with a look of horror. Suddenly, all his joy disappeared. He felt very nervous.

He turned to Lin. The expression on her face made him feel even worse. She looked unbelievably sad.

"Mother, this is Daniel," she said, her voice shaking. "We met at leadership camp."

Daniel made a tentative move to shake hands, but Mrs. Park drew back. Without a word, she turned and left the hallway.

Daniel turned back to Lin. She had her hand over her mouth, her eyes were closed, and she was shaking her head.

"Are — are you okay?" he asked. He was totally bewildered. This was hardly the reception he'd expected.

"Come outside," Lin whispered, and Daniel followed her.

"What's going on?" he asked. "Why did your mother look at me like that?"

"Oh, Daniel," Lin moaned, "why didn't you listen to me? I told you to be patient. I told you I needed time before I could see you again."

"I waited a week — " Daniel began, but Lin wouldn't let him finish.

"A week isn't enough! Daniel, don't you realize what you've done? You've ruined everything!"

Daniel felt like he was losing his mind. "What do you mean?" he asked wildly.

"I hadn't even told my parents about you yet. I was working up to it, telling them about all the nice people I met at camp. I knew they would have a hard time accepting the idea of my dating a boy — especially a boy who is not Asian. I had to bring up the idea slowly, carefully, preparing them to meet you."

Tears welled in her eyes. "Daniel, I've hurt my mother terribly. Do you have any idea what she must have thought when she saw you kissing me in the hallway? Daniel, she'll never accept you now!"

Slowly, the significance of what Lin was saying hit him. He gazed at her steadily.

"What about you?"

Now the tears were trickling down her cheeks. "I can't see you again, Daniel. Never again." Giving him one last devastated look, she turned and ran back inside the house.

Daniel just stood there, frozen. Then, like a robot, he went to his car, got inside, and started the engine. Her words echoed in his ears. Never again. Never again.

And as the meaning of those words penetrated his brain, he found out what heartbreak really meant.

Coming soon . . .

Couples #35

BREAK AWAY

Torrey cleared his throat and edged closer to Sara on the bench. "I'm glad you're not in a hurry." Torrey swallowed hard. "I mean, it's hard to get to know somebody when you only see them where they work."

Sara laughed a little. She didn't seem to mind that he was sitting so close to her.

"I know what you mean," she replied. "It's hard enough to know what to say and how to act when you see each other at school or something."

Uneasily, Torrey nodded. Suddenly he wasn't so sure he wanted Sara to know what he was like. What if she found out that he hung out at the Hall of Shame and that his whole life was a screwed-up mess? She'd never like him if she knew. Warily, he said, "Maybe it won't be worth the effort to learn about me. Maybe you'll find out you really hate me."

"No," she said, "it's *always* worth the effort to

get to know somebody." She half turned on the bench to face him, and there was another silence. Then she added, almost in a whisper, "Especially if it's somebody you already like a lot." Her voice trembled a little.

Sara turned to look at him, her face serene in the moonlight, her lips parted to speak. Torrey felt a surge of emotions well up inside him. He touched his hand gently to her cheek, and his arm tightened around her shoulders, pulling her closer to him. For a long moment they looked at each other, and then he bent to kiss her. They were both stiff at first, uncertain. But then, tentatively, Sara put her arms around his neck and melted into his arms. Torrey held her tightly, feeling dizzy with happiness.

True love!   Crushes!   Breakups!   Makeups!

Read about the excitement–and heartache–of being part of a *couple*!

Order these titles today!

- ☐ 33390-9   #1   **CHANGE OF HEARTS** Linda A. Cooney
- ☐ 33391-7   #2   **FIRE AND ICE** Linda A. Cooney
- ☐ 33392-5   #3   **ALONE TOGETHER** Linda A. Cooney
- ☐ 33393-3   #4   **MADE FOR EACH OTHER** M.E. Cooper
- ☐ 33394-1   #5   **MOVING TOO FAST** M.E. Cooper
- ☐ 33395-X   #6   **CRAZY LOVE** M.E. Cooper
- ☐ 40238-2   #15 **COMING ON STRONG** M.E. Cooper
- ☐ 40239-0   #16 **SWEETHEARTS** M.E. Cooper
- ☐ 40240-4   #17 **DANCE WITH ME** M.E. Cooper
- ☐ 40422-9   #18 **KISS AND RUN** M.E. Cooper
- ☐ 40424-5   #19 **SHOW SOME EMOTION** M.E. Cooper
- ☐ 40425-3   #20 **NO CONTEST** M.E. Cooper
- ☐ 40426-1   #21 **TEACHER'S PET** M.E. Cooper
- ☐ 40427-X   #22 **SLOW DANCING** M.E. Cooper
- ☐ 40792-9   #23 **BYE BYE LOVE** M.E. Cooper
- ☐ 40794-5   #24 **SOMETHING NEW** M.E. Cooper
- ☐ 40795-3   #25 **LOVE EXCHANGE** M.E. Cooper
- ☐ 40796-1   #26 **HEAD OVER HEELS** M.E. Cooper
- ☐ 40797-X   #27 **SWEET AND SOUR** M.E. Cooper
- ☐ 41262-0   #28 **LOVESTRUCK** M.E. Cooper

Complete series available wherever you buy books. $2.50 each

**Scholastic Inc., P.O. Box 7502, 2932 East McCarty Street
Jefferson City, MO 65102**

Please send me the books I have checked above. I am enclosing $_____
(please add $1.00 to cover shipping and handling). Send check or money order–
no cash or C.O.D.'s please.

Name_____

Address_____

City_____State/Zip_____

Please allow four to six weeks for delivery. Offer good in U.S.A. only. Sorry, mail-order not available to residents of
Canada. Prices subject to change.   COU987